ACCIDENTAL ARCHAEOLOGIST

HALF-WIZARD THORDRIC BOOK 2

KATHRYN WELLS

For all those who were told their dreams were impossible to achieve.

1

LIGHT AS A FEATHER

High Wizard Vey levitated the giant cauldron into the centre of the room, careful not to spill the boiling water inside it onto the floor. Flicking his shoulder-length black hair out of his eyes, he set it down and pulled out a handful of strange plants from the pockets of his sapphire-coloured robes.

As he sorted through them and separated them out into specific piles, Thordric, who was watching from behind, frowned slightly. He was quite the potion maker himself and so knew some highly unusual plants, but he had never seen any of these ones before. One in particular he wasn't even sure *was* a plant; it looked as though it had been carved out of stone.

Vey smiled as he saw Thordric staring. 'It's been petrified,' he said, handing the plant to him so he could have a closer look. 'It's like a fossil, though I had to use magic to speed up the process. It has to be like that for the potion to work.' He laughed and shook his head. 'Honestly, you should have seen the time I used it fresh. It turned my hair and beard into feathers.'

Usually Thordric would have laughed too, but today all he managed was a weak smile. Vey raised his eyebrow.

'So, what exactly is this potion supposed to do? When you've got it right, I mean?' Thordric said, avoiding Vey's gaze.

Vey had been instructing him for three years now, ever since Thordric had become the youngest member of the Wizard Council at only fifteen. That was after Thordric had solved the mystery of the previous High Wizard's death and Vey had taken his place.

The Wizard Council had been very different back then, not just in the products it produced but also its policies and prejudices too. Only full wizards, which meant those who had been born from a family with no previous wizards in them, could become members of the council. Half-wizards like Thordric and, unknown to everyone at the time, Vey, had been looked down upon as having weak and dangerous magic. No one trusted them and as Thordric had discovered, the previous High Wizard had wanted them all stamped out for good.

Vey grinned, the movement making his short, tufted beard part down the middle. 'It's supposed to create a feeling of weightlessness. I began developing it for mother, actually, since she's starting to get arthritis. I thought it would help her move around more easily. If it works for her, I may even put it on our product line so that all older people can use it.'

Thordric blinked. He had never thought of Lizzie, Vey's mother, as old. She had been the one who had first taught him how to control his magic, though she had no magic herself.

That was one of the unsolved mysteries of magic; there had never been a single woman who had been born with it in all the history of the land. Thordric thought that was a terrible shame, for Lizzie would have made a wonderful job of it.

'But Lizzie's not old enough to get arthritis,' he objected.

'Mother is very deceptive in her looks, Thordric. I assure

2

you she is no less than sixty. But arthritis does run in our family. It doesn't affect solely the elderly though; my grandmother developed it at the age of thirty-five.'

By this time, Vey had carefully cut up the important parts of each plant and placed them into the cauldron, creating a greenish mixture which stood bubbling away quite pleasantly. A light blue steam began to rise from it as Vey stirred alternately clockwise and counterclockwise. That was the trick to potions. They all had such strict ways of stirring that Thordric thought he would never master some of the more advanced ones. Then again, as Vey always reminded him, he had never believed he would be able to master any of his magic.

'It should be done in a moment,' Vey said after about twenty minutes. 'Would you help me drain it?'

Only the liquid part of a potion was ever used, sort of like making tea, so all the bits of plant had to be sieved out before it was drinkable.

Thordric picked up a large, round mat of weaved rushes and put it over the cauldron. Then he found a large cooking pot and levitated it across the room so that it stood next to the cauldron, ready for the liquid to be poured into it.

'Right,' Vey said, his brow sweating slightly from the steam. 'You tip and I'll make sure the mat stays in place.'

Without touching it, Thordric tipped the cauldron gently over while Vey stuck the mat to it like a lid with his magic. The liquid, now blue like the steam, came pouring out and into the cooking pot. Once it was done, Vey fetched two goblets and filled them both with the potion.

'Care to have a taste?' he said, offering a goblet to Thordric.

Thordric eyed the goblet warily, remembering what Vey had said about ending up with feathers instead of hair, but quickly put it out of his mind. Vey had been working on this potion for three weeks now, nothing like that should happen again. He took the goblet and drank it all in one gulp, feeling as if he had swallowed an entire stagnant pond.

'Why is it that all good potions taste so awful?' he complained, realising that his body really did feel lighter. It was so light, in fact, that the breeze from the open window was pushing him back slightly.

Vey tugged at his beard as he too found himself being pushed back by the gentle breeze. 'Hmm, I suppose I'll have to work on it a bit more. It won't do any good to have people being blown away by a simple puff of wind.'

He went to tip the potion away, but then Thordric called out to him.

'Wait, Vey. It seems to be settling down now. The feeling is still there, but I'm not being pushed back. It needs a few minutes to work properly, that's all.'

Vey realised it was true, his muscles relaxing with relief. 'Would you like to come with me to mother's and see what she thinks of it?' he asked.

Thordric thought of Lizzie being pushed around her garden by the wind. He couldn't resist.

Lizzie was in a dreadful mood when they arrived, having just caught her skirt on a rosebush she had been pruning.

'Well, now that you're both here, I suppose you want supper,' she said, hardly sparing them a glance as she looked at the large tear on her skirt.

'Actually, we were here to—'

Thordric nudged Vey in the ribs. Though Vey was her son, he had run away when he was only sixteen and not seen her again for over ten years. He struggled to read her moods still, but Thordric knew her better. Lizzie liked company when she was in a bad mood and, what's more, she knew that they could mend her skirt in moments if she asked them to. Thordric thought he would offer first.

'I'll fix your skirt for you if you like,' he said. She beamed at him.

Thordric ran his hand down the soft fabric, feeling the tear and picturing it weaving itself back together, even stronger than it had been before. He was good at this sort of magic, for it was this kind that Lizzie had first set him to learning; fixing an old, battered kettle that was now whistling away merrily on the stove. He felt like patting it affectionately but thought better of it.

Standing up, with Lizzie's skirt in one piece again, he saw Vey tipping the potion into a glass behind Lizzie's back. He sighed. Vey really lacked tact.

'I know what you're up to, Eric,' she said sharply, turning to Vey. Thordric laughed inwardly at her use of Vey's real name. No matter how much he heard it, he couldn't get used to it.

'At least let me have some cake ready so that I can deal with whatever foul taste that one has,' she continued, pulling a face. 'The last two left me feeling something dreadful.'

Vey put the glass he had been about to offer her down somewhat guiltily. Lizzie waved her hand at the table and told them to sit down while she cut them all some cake and poured the tea.

Thordric noticed sadly that Vey was right; her movements were so stiff and laboured that he thought arthritis could be the only cause.

'Lizzie,' he said, taking a gulp of tea. 'Why didn't you tell me you had arthritis?'

'Arthritis? Is that what Eric's been telling you?' she said, casting a nasty glance in Vey's direction. Vey paled visibly.

'Mother, you know it's arthritis. There's no shame in it,' he said quietly.

Lizzie snorted as she took a seat. 'If it was arthritis, then it would be consistent. I only get like this every other day. Unfortunately, you had to see me on one of them.'

'Then what's causing it?' Thordric said, now taking a large lump of cake.

'I'm not really sure, boy. It started about five weeks ago after I went to visit my dear sister-in-law. I admit it was a long journey, but I wouldn't have thought it would have caused any lasting damage.' She tightened her bun of hair, making her look rather like a stern schoolteacher, and turned her attention back to Vey. 'Well, I suppose I had better drink whatever it is you've got for me this time.'

Vey handed her the glass and she looked at the potion critically, sniffing it before she even thought of drinking. 'At least it has a pleasant aroma,' she said, and drank it in a single go as Thordric had.

Vey and Thordric watched her closely. She looked back at them and ate a hasty slice of cake.

'Well?' Vey said after a moment. 'How do you feel?'

'I feel as though a good gust of wind would blow me away,' she said and, glancing at her open window as it got further and further away, added, 'and I do believe it is.'

Thordric caught hold of her chair to stop it moving back any further. 'That part wears off in a moment,' he said, hoping that it still would. Vey gave her an encouraging look, and Thordric noticed he was sweating again.

Lizzie sipped her tea, then stood up. 'You're right,' she said, doing a girlish twirl. 'I must say, Eric, it's certainly done the job this time.'

She walked around the room, her usual light and graceful movement returning more by the moment. 'Honestly, I feel so light that I could dance on water. Though,' she added darkly, 'I would do something about the taste before you start selling it to the public. Perhaps a dash of mint would do the trick. I have some growing in the garden, you know.'

Thordric caught the hint and got up to pick some while Vey groaned.

There was a small patch of it outside the back door. He picked half and took it in. Lizzie and Vey's conversation switched off quickly as he entered the room.

'Vey was telling me that you seem a bit down of late, boy,' Lizzie said, thrusting yet another slice of cake in his direction. 'Would you care to tell me why?'

Thordric didn't care to, but it would do no good not to say. 'I...' he began, but his throat had grown dry. He felt so terribly guilty about it all.

Taking another gulp of tea, he started again. 'I've been part of the council for three years now and I've learnt a lot thanks to both of you,' he said, his palms growing hot. 'But I feel as though I haven't done anything useful yet. Everyone is working on something except for me.'

'That's not true,' Vey said, frowning at him. 'What about that potion you made that stops bleeding? I know you haven't finished it yet, but it's almost there.'

'That was an accident,' Thordric said, looking down. 'I was trying to develop a new fertiliser for the trees in the council garden, but I knocked over two of the batches I'd made, and they mixed together in a sticky mess. That potion was the result.'

Vey couldn't help but smile, but his face dropped as Thordric glared at him. 'Well,' he said, gulping slightly, 'you've got to find something that you truly care about. Everything the council does now is a direct result of wanting to make things better for everyone. Like this potion. I would never have made it if I hadn't wanted to help mother out, yet now I have something that will help many more people.'

'So, I should think of something that I want to change for the better?' Thordric asked.

Vey nodded. 'Just because I'm teaching you doesn't mean that you're not free to pursue something of your own. All I want to do is help you when you have need of it.'

'My, my, Eric, how awfully grown up of you,' Lizzie said to Vey slyly. She turned to Thordric. 'He's right, boy. It's up to you to find what it is you want to do, but whatever it is, you'll have our support all the way.'

2

THE BEGINNINGS OF A PLAN

The station house was insufferably warm as Thordric made his way to Inspector Jimmson's office. As he passed, the constables, busy working at their desks, dipped their heads to him respectfully. No matter how much time passed, he still found it strange to think that he no longer had to run the inspector's errands now that he was part of the Wizard Council instead of a lowly runner at the station.

It had been nearly three years since Jimmson had married Thordric's mother, but despite that and his new twin baby sisters, Thordric couldn't help but think of him as an inspector first and his stepfather second.

He reached the door and knocked politely before going in. The inspector was sitting in his chair, facing away, and he appeared to be making strange cooing sounds. Thordric raised an eyebrow and coughed.

The inspector turned around quickly, his arms held protectively over Thordric's baby sisters, frowning so much that his eyebrows met in the middle. However, that wasn't what made Thordric snort the most. Inspector Jimmson was known for

9

having a large, emotionally responsive moustache. On this occasion, however, it appeared to be half missing.

'Now, there's no need to laugh, boy,' the inspector said, anxiously glancing at the windows to see if any of the constables were looking in. They weren't. 'You should have seen the trouble I went through this morning trying to get in without anyone noticing.'

Thordric snorted again and his sisters gurgled at him happily. 'What happened?' he asked, taking Elle, the slightly bigger of the two. Her sister, Mae, scowled at her and dribbled over the inspector's hand.

'Look in her hand,' the inspector replied, gesturing to Elle.

Thordric looked down at Elle's tightly clenched pudgy fist and gently prized it open. Inside was a handful of stiff brown hairs, matching the inspector's moustache. Thordric laughed and the inspector shushed him impatiently.

'Well, boy,' he said. 'Can you grow it back again?'

'Of course I can,' Thordric said. 'I did it before, didn't I?'

He handed Elle back to the inspector and looked at his moustache, picturing the hair growing back while willing it to do so. It started growing almost immediately, catching up with the other side. Before it could get too long, however, Thordric stopped it. He pulled a mirror out of his pocket and held it up for the inspector to see. The inspector turned his head from side to side, looking at his moustache from all angles. Satisfied, he let out a large sigh which caused Elle and Mae to gurgle at him.

'Thank you, boy. Now I can stop hiding from everyone. You, er, won't tell anyone about this, will you?' he said, bobbing the twins up and down on his knees. Elle, spotting the new hair growth, was already reaching up to grab it again but she couldn't quite get it. Instead, she made herself content with teething on the inspector's tie. Mae saw her and started chewing the other side.

'I won't say a word, not even to mother,' Thordric promised. 'I suppose she's working today, seeing as you have the girls?' he asked.

'Yes, she's in the morgue now. Two unexplained deaths came in this morning needing post-mortem examinations if I recall. Honestly, I can't fathom how she does it. And to think she uses those same hands to make dinner of an evening.' The inspector shook his head, turning a little pale.

'You get used to it after a while,' Thordric lied.

His mother had her hands buried in the latest poor soul's chest when he entered the morgue.

'Thordric, what a pleasant surprise. Has Vey given you some time off?' she said, wiping her hands on her apron and passing him a mug of tea. He took it, carefully avoiding the part that she had touched and took a sip. It tasted of blueberries and chocolate, a new blend made by the Wizard Council, if he was not mistaken.

'I suppose you could put it that way. He told me to find something I'm passionate about, but I can't think of anything.'

'Well, what is it for?' she asked, her hands back in her victim. Thordric averted his eyes.

'I said I wanted something useful to do,' he said.

'Useful in what way?' she said. Alarmingly, she picked up some type of saw and began hacking at the body with it. Thordric looked desperately into his teacup, trying to ignore the sound of metal grinding on bone.

'That's just it, I'm not sure,' he said. 'Vey keeps coming up with potions to help with different ailments, Wizard Batsu has developed a new type of plant that disperses bad odours and refreshes everything with its scent and Wizard Myak is the one who is developing all these new tea blends that give different benefits depending on the flavour. I don't know how to compete with that.'

'Then don't,' his mother said, shrugging as she put down the saw and looked critically at what she'd done. 'Listen, Thordric. You and Vey have been working together trying to make the council a better place than it was when Kalljard was there. Why don't you use your passion for that to help you figure out what to do?' she said.

Thordric stared at her without blinking. 'Mother, you're a genius!' he said, getting up and splashing tea down his front.

'I'm glad you think so,' she replied, now picking up a dangerously sharp metal instrument and plunging it deep into the body. Thordric suddenly felt the need to stretch his legs.

'There's a cloth over there that you can dry yourself off with on your way out,' she added, without looking up.

Thordric took it and hurriedly left the room.

He walked back to the Wizard Council's turquoise, crescent-moon-shaped building, striding straight past the giant main doors and around to the back, where a single small door was set into the wall. He pulled a silver key from his pocket, emblazoned with the new Council emblem: a book and potion bottle in front of a silver half-moon.

That had been Thordric's idea, his way of letting people see that the council had changed. The book and potion bottle had been the old symbol, but he had added the silver half-moon as a tribute to Vey's father, whose methods they now used to train young wizards, including half-wizards.

He unlocked the door and went in, passing the dormitories of the lower-level wizards and making his way up to Vey's room at the very top of the building. Vey opened the door before he could even knock and beckoned him in.

'So,' he said, handing Thordric a plate of cold meat and fruits. Thordric took it gladly, realising that he had missed dinner in the serving halls. 'What was it that my dear Uncle wanted?'

The inspector, as well as being Thordric's stepfather, was also Lizzie's brother, therefore making he and Vey like cousins. Thordric had always been comfortable with that arrangement, for Vey and Lizzie had been like family ever since he had known them. He thought Vey rather liked it too, after not having much of a family for so long.

'He had a bit of trouble with his moustache,' he replied. 'One of the twins had pulled half of it out.'

Vey laughed. 'I think your sisters are going to be very lively as they get older.'

'They're lively now,' Thordric said with a grin. 'Mother seems to be able to handle them well, though.'

He ate everything on his plate, absently levitating a large crystal ball between himself and Vey in an unusual game of catch. When he had finished, Vey looked at him seriously. 'Have you given any thought to what I said earlier?' he said. 'I feel awful when you get all gloomy like that.'

To his surprise, Thordric smiled. 'Actually, I have. There's a lot of wizards who refused to be part of the council before you took over, aren't there?'

'You mean the Wanderers?' Vey asked, interested.

'The very same. I thought I would find them and let them know what happened. I could also find other half-wizards and tell them about our training.'

Vey sat back in his chair, tugging at his beard again. Thordric wondered how he hadn't pulled it out by now. 'It's not quite what I was thinking, but it's definitely a worthy cause.

We've got a few records of them somewhere; nothing detailed mind, but I think they mention the location they were last at.'

'Kalljard kept records of them?' Thordric asked.

'Of course he did. You know as well as I what a suspicious man he was. I think being High Wizard for nearly a thousand years went to his head.'

Thordric had to agree; Kalljard had certainly been a nasty piece of work.

'Come with me, I believe the records are now in the library,' Vey said, getting up. 'I need your help down there, sometime,' he added. 'You've worked with Father's books more than I have; I'm afraid I don't know which section to put them in.'

The library was bathed in a warm red glow from the floating fires along the walls. Thordric had wondered whether it was safe to have fires like that around the books at first, but Vey had assured him that they wouldn't actually burn anything.

'Now, let's see, where would it be?' Vey said, scanning the shelves for the section names.

'Maybe under *Distant Towns*?' Thordric hastened a guess. If, as their name suggested, they really did wander, then he supposed they wouldn't still be anywhere near Jard Town. He went over to the travelling section, finding the *Distant Towns* subsection a short way in. There, in front of him, was a thin, velvet-covered folder with a black label attached to it, with the word 'Wanderers' written on it in red ink. Snatching it up, he took it back to Vey.

'Ah, you found it,' he said as Thordric handed it to him. He put it on a table, carefully unwrapping the velvet cloth to reveal the leather-bound folder underneath. Opening it, among a great cloud of dust, they found a map and a few names written in faded ink on a small piece of paper.

'Now,' Vey continued, unfolding the map, and spreading it full out on the table. 'As you know, all the wizards of the council and the Wizard Council Training Facility live here in town.' He pointed to a dot on the map labelled Jard Town. 'No Wanderers would have dared to stay here in case they were caught, so...'

They both scanned the map. In the top right corner, in a place called Neathin Valley, was a cluster of red dots, much like ants. He counted seven.

Thordric counted the list of names; there were also seven. 'They must be here, look,' he told Vey, showing him the names and dots.

'Neathin Valley? I've never been there for myself, but I've heard some strange rumours about the place. I'm sure my father's sister used to live there.'

'Didn't Lizzie say that she visited her sister-in-law fairly recently? Perhaps I could ask her about it,' Thordric said, rather excitedly.

'Yes, if my aunt still lives there.' Vey looked at the large clock in the room, its pendulum floating rather than swinging. 'Let's go back to my chambers. It's not altogether safe to be here after hours, not even for me. Wizard Callus will be furious if he catches anyone lingering here with his precious books still out of place, High Wizard or not.'

Thordric agreed heartily. He had once had the misfortune to spill ink over a book he had borrowed. The word 'imbecile' that Wizard Callus had magically stamped all over his body hadn't come off for six weeks.

Once they were safely in Vey's chambers, they spread the map out again on the floor. 'So, how do I get there?' Thordric asked, looking at the distance between Jard Town and Neathin Valley. It was nearly two thousand miles. 'I can't take a carriage all that way.'

'Of course not,' Vey laughed. 'You'll have to travel by floating ship.'

'You mean the floating Ships of Kal?' Thordric gasped. He knew that the late High Wizard Kalljard had created them over five hundred years ago, but he had never even set eyes on one before.

'The very same,' Vey said. 'Kalljard had very few good ideas, but those ships were definitely one of them.'

'But I thought that boarding one cost over a year's worth of wages?'

'It did,' Vey said. 'Until I found out how they really work. You see, everyone thought that the magic used on them was terribly advanced and took a lot of energy, so a large fee was at least somewhat acceptable. However, not long after Kalljard... departed, I had a chance to go on one.'

'And?' Thordric asked, fascinated.

'It was nothing more than a compound of minerals and herbs, rather like a potion, in fact, used as fuel. I was terribly disappointed to find out that all of the ingredients were as easy to obtain as the ones we use in our simple potions.'

'How much is it now?' Thordric asked.

'Six coins each way, including cabins and food. Of course, you won't have to pay anything seeing as you're going on official business,' he said smugly. 'Now, get to bed and we'll discuss it all in the morning.'

3

DIGGING AWAY

Thordric rose early that morning, far too early to see Vey, who never awoke until breakfast was ready. Instead, he thought about his travelling plans and realised that he had no way of communicating with Vey or Lizzie while he was away. What if something didn't quite go to plan? He could get lost or the Wanderers might reject him, or worse...

There must be something he could use to send messages back and forth. He had heard of a number of stones that had powerful connective powers, but he had never been much good at using rocks and minerals. Plants were more his style, but was it possible to use one to communicate?

He thought back to when he had helped Lizzie in the garden last. She had said something about being able to separate a single plant into two or more parts if it was starting to get too big. Perhaps if he found the right plant, the separated pieces could still be linked together. All he would have to do would be to make it possible for his voice to travel from one piece to the other. That way, he could give one each to Vey and Lizzie and keep another for himself.

Searching through his rather limited collection of books, he found a small, neatly handwritten one. It was an encyclopaedia of plants, written by Vey's father and though it had been a while since he'd read it, Thordric was sure that there had been something about a plant which aided communication.

He flicked through it, glancing past the neat hand-drawn pictures showing what the plants looked like and listing their rarity and uses. It wasn't *Big Man's Nose,* it definitely wasn't *Winsome Sunbeam,* nor *Hedra Laxa, Ratel Arba, Glorious Poom...*

The list went on, but still he couldn't find it. He was sure it had been here somewhere.

Wait. Near the back, a page had been torn out. He could see that whoever had taken it had been somewhat hasty, as the remaining part was so jagged that it looked like a set of teeth.

He shut the book with an aggressive snap and went up to see if Vey was awake yet. If someone was stealing, it should be reported. Of all things, it had to be the page that he needed...

Once up the spiral stairs to Vey's tower room, he knocked on the door, far harder than he was intending. There was a loud, rather startled shout from inside and the heavy sound of footsteps.

'Hello?' Vey said, his head appearing around the door. His dark hair and beard were a mess, and his eyes were squinted from the light. 'Oh, Thordric, it's you.'

He opened the door a bit more and let Thordric in. Thordric noticed with amusement that not only was Vey wearing husky pink night robes, he was also sporting acid-green socks. Thordric had always felt sleeping with socks on was a most curious habit and would have said so if he'd not still been angry.

'Would you like some tea?' Vey asked, offering a cup he had just summoned from the kitchens.

'Thank you,' Thordric said, taking it. Tea would be good, particularly if it was the blend which calmed the drinker down after a single sip. He didn't want to take his anger out on Vey, particularly when he was in such a sleepy state, for he would simply go back to bed and zoom Thordric's chair out of the room.

'What is it you woke me up for?' Vey said, after Thordric had drunk some. He was awake enough to notice Thordric's mood and had poured him an extra cup in case the first was not enough.

Immediately Thordric felt better, but the question now made him feel guilty for not waiting until later in the day. 'A page from one of my books has been torn out,' he said quietly.

Vey frowned, tugging at his beard again and noticing that it had somehow become tangled with his hair. 'Which book was it? One of Father's?'

'Yes, it was the plant encyclopaedia. I was looking for a particular plant, but when I went to look for it, the page was gone.'

To his surprise, Vey started chuckling and went over to his drawers. He opened the first one and pulled out a sheet of paper, with jagged edges on one side. 'Is this it?' he asked.

Thordric took it and looked. It was.

'And I thought I had a bad memory,' Vey continued, still chuckling. 'You gave that to me weeks ago to look at, something about using it in a potion to create psychic ability.'

Thordric felt rather silly. He *did* remember.

'I, er...thanks,' he said.

'So,' Vey said, curious now. 'What did you want it for this time? It must have been something exciting if you were looking for it this early.'

Thordric winced as a fresh layer of guilt fell onto him.

Nevertheless, he explained his idea. Vey listened, occasionally nodding, though mostly trying to untangle his beard.

'Let me see if I've understood you,' he said, finally getting the last of his hair free from his beard. 'You want to divide a single plant into three, keeping it alive, so that each person who has one is linked with the other two?'

'Yes,' Thordric replied.

'Then, you might be onto something there. Take a look at this,' Vey said, digging around in his drawer again. 'Ah, here it is.'

He pulled out a wad of notes, transcribed in the same writing as Thordric's book. Vey's father had written them, then. 'This is...!' he began, scanning the first page. 'It's almost exactly what I had in mind, though I admit I wasn't sure how to make voices carry across.'

'You want to work on it?' Vey said, smiling as he saw Thordric's excitement.

'Of course. With this, I'll be able to speak to you when I'm in Neathin Valley.' Thordric's grin was so large that he was positively beaming.

'Good. Now, if you don't mind, I'm going back to bed. Never did me any good getting up early...'

Thordric left him to it.

The plant Thordric needed was called *Tenro Aqus* and, despite having magical properties, was generally used as a table flower in cafe's and sometimes at home. But Thordric needed more than just the flowers, he needed the roots. If he didn't separate the plant at the roots, then it wouldn't work.

The only place where he knew they grew wild in town was the graveyard.

With a sigh, Thordric dressed himself in his official robes and, after a hurried breakfast, made his way there.

There was a fog that morning, but with it came a crisp freshness that Thordric found rather soothing. Unfortunately, the fog was so thick that he missed the graveyard entrance twice and had to keep circling back.

When he finally got there, he had to push the fog away from the graves with one of his spells, for the *Tenro Aqus* only grew by two of them. He found them quickly, greeted by a clump of luminous blue flowers, each one no bigger than his thumb. Only then did it dawn on him that he had forgotten to bring a spade.

Never mind; the groundkeeper would have one.

Putting up a red marker so that he could find the *Tenro Aqus* again without having to shift the fog, he made his way to the groundkeeper's shed. He found it locked, but with a trick he had learnt from Vey, summoned a spade from within. It didn't go quite as he'd planned, however, for instead of it simply appearing in his hand, it levitated itself through the window with such a crash that several birds took to flight.

Thordric winced but put the thought aside. He could fix it later. For now, he had a plant to dig up.

It was nearing midday by the time that Thordric got back to his chambers, carrying a large clump of *Tenro Aqus,* and covered in earth. He had never thought that a plant could put up such a fight when trying to be dug up. No sooner had he put the spade in the ground than the plant disappeared and popped up again a few metres away, waving its blue flowers at him almost mockingly.

In the end, Thordric had to trick it into believing he was digging for something else. It was a difficult piece of magic, for he had to dig in one place but make the force of the spade impact another, so that he was actually digging around the plant without having to stand near it. It had left him weak and tired, but it'd worked.

He would have to tell Lizzie about that one, for, being his first teacher, she loved to hear about the kinds of magic he was doing. Particularly if it was something complicated.

It was then that he remembered that he wanted to speak with her about Neathin Valley. He thought about asking Vey if he wanted to go too, but then remembered his earlier intrusion and decided against it.

The fog had all but cleared now and, having put the *Tenro Aqus* somewhere safe where he thought it couldn't get away, he made his way to Lizzie's townhouse.

She was in the garden when he arrived, taking snippets of rosehip and dandelion. Seeing him coming, she wiped her hands on her apron and opened the door for him, frowning slightly as he walked mud into the hall.

'What brings you here again, boy?' she asked, still frowning.

Thordric realised why and hastily sent all the mud from the carpet and himself back to the graveyard where it should have been. Lizzie smiled instantly.

'There was something I wanted to ask you. Have you ever been to Neathin Valley?'

'I have, though not too far in. I believe I told you that I went to visit my sister-in-law a few weeks ago. Neathin Valley is where she lives.'

So, Vey had been right.

'Could you tell me about it?' he asked, absently taking a biscuit from the plateful that she was offering.

'There's not an awful lot to say, boy,' she said, her brow

creased. 'Neathin Valley is a very dry place, with only one town called Valley Edge. It actually runs along the edge of the valley, not in it, and there are a lot of underground springs a few miles out in what is known as the Valley Flats. I believe people bathe in them to help recover from mild illnesses, though I wasn't fortunate to go to one myself. It's said that men and women bathe together there.'

Thordric's cheeks went rather pink at this but swallowed his embarrassment down with his biscuit. 'Did you notice any wizards around?'

'Wizards? I didn't know there were any there. Did Eric send some over?' she asked.

'Not yet,' he said. 'But I was going to go there.'

She studied him, curious. 'What's this all about, boy?'

'I've decided to find the Wanderers. They don't know about the council's reform, you see.'

'So, you wanted to let them know so that they could join if they wanted? It will take you some time to convince them,' she said. 'From what I've heard, they're rather distrustful of anyone from the council.'

'I'm not surprised. Vey and I discovered that Kalljard had been tracking them for a long time. We've even got the names of some of them.'

'Really? How fascinating. Though given Kalljard's paranoid disposition, it's no wonder,' she said, offering him another biscuit. 'Now, would you care to explain to me why you were covered in mud?'

Thordric told her about his plans for his communication device and about his trouble with the *Tenro Aqus*. Much to his disgust, she laughed throughout the whole thing. And, he realised, he had forgotten to fix the broken window on the groundkeeper's shed.

'Never mind, boy,' she said, still laughing. 'You can fix it later.'

She stood up and went to put on some more tea. Thordric thought for a moment and then choked on his biscuit. If she had really been to Neathin Valley, then she must have gone on one of the Ships of Kal. He had to ask her about it!

4

THE LONG-DISTANCE
COMMUNICATOR

By following the plans that Vey's father had put down in his notes and by trying a few things out for himself, Thordric finally announced that his long-distance communication device was ready.

'Shall we test it?' he asked Vey, who had snuck one into Lizzie's townhouse earlier that day.

'I think so,' Vey said. He pushed a button on the small wooden box in front of him, out of which a single blue flower was poking. 'Do I just speak to it like this?'

Thordric nodded. 'Try saying something loudly, I'm not sure how the volume will be at her end.'

'Alright,' Vey replied. He coughed, readying his voice. 'MOTHER? MOTHER, ARE YOU THERE?'

Thordric winced. Even the blue flower had dipped down out of sight. 'Perhaps not quite so loud after all,' he said, tapping the box gently so that the flower bobbed back up again.

Vey repeated himself, not quite so thunderous this time.

'Eric? Eric, is that you?' Lizzie's voice came out of the box, as clear as if she were standing in the room. 'It appears as though you've turned yourself into some sort of plant.'

Thordric snorted, so hard that it made him sneeze.

'Is that you, boy?' Lizzie said. 'What's happened? Why can I hear you both coming out of this...contraption?'

Trying to control himself, Thordric explained.

'My, my, boy,' she said when he was done. 'You've outdone yourself this time. Though I must say, Neathin Valley is a lot further away than my house, you know. Are you sure it will work over that great a distance?'

Thordric didn't have the faintest idea as to whether it would or not. Even so, he had created something useful after all. Perhaps he should demonstrate it to the inspector. He had to visit his mother anyway to let her know that he would be leaving soon, so he could do it while he was there.

He arrived at his mother's and the inspector's house a few hours later, bearing a large platter of food in one hand and the communication device in the other. The platter was so heavy that he'd to use a levitation spell in order to carry it there, but it had been necessary to bring it because, talented as his mother was in the morgue, her cooking tended to burst into flames all too frequently.

The door opened before he even pulled the bell and he found himself greeted by his mother holding the twins. 'Thordy! Thordy,' they gurgled at him, reaching out to grab the newly grown beard on his chin.

He increased the levitation spell on the platter so that it whizzed over their heads and landed on the dining table so he could take a twin in each arm. Hastily, he tucked the delicate communication device into his pocket so that they wouldn't try to pull out the flower and sever the roots inside.

'It's nice to see you again, Thordric,' his mother said, inviting him in. 'You don't visit anywhere near enough.'

He winced, not at her words, but at the twins as they both grabbed hold of his beard and tugged hard, each coming away with a handful of hair.

His mother didn't even try to tell them off. 'Honestly, Thordric, I don't understand why you feel the need to keep growing it. You look much more handsome without it.'

Thordric flushed as he saw the inspector watching him, his great, bushy moustache dancing about on his upper lip with mirth.

'I'm hungry,' he said, hastily changing the subject. 'Shall we eat?'

They sat around the table, his mother serving everyone large helpings of meat and hot spiced vegetables from the platter that Thordric had brought. Somehow, Thordric had been left holding the twins, which meant that while he was eating, he had to levitate them into the air to stop them tugging at his fork. They thought it was enormous fun, particularly when they found themselves close enough to the chandelier to swing from it.

Unfortunately, Thordric hadn't noticed and so ended up with a shower of crystal prisms bouncing off his head.

'Perhaps I should take them for a moment?' his mother suggested as another lot rained down on him. Thordric agreed readily but had to carefully prize their chubby fingers open with magic before he could get them down.

Once they had finished eating and the twins had been put to bed, Thordric took out his long-distance communicator and placed it on the coffee table.

'Fancy yourself as a horticulturalist, boy?' the inspector jibed, noticing the flower poking happily out of the top.

'Now, now, Jimmson, don't make fun of him,' Thordric's

mother said, sitting down with them. 'Though I have to say, Thordric, that is a terribly curious-looking flower. I presume you have an explanation?'

Thordric opened his mouth to reply, but Vey's voice answered for him. 'He most certainly does, Maggie.'

The inspector, who had been drinking his coffee at the time, replied by spraying it all down his front. 'What in Spell's name? That was High Wizard Vey speaking!' he said, his moustache curling up to his nostrils.

'Ah, forgive me, Inspector,' Vey's voice came from the communicator. 'It was not my intention to startle you. What you're hearing is my voice being transported from my chambers into the small device in front of you. It was invented by your stepson, with a little help from my father's notes.'

'But what exactly is it for?' the inspector asked, his moustache relaxing back down. 'With respect, your reverence, I don't believe that scaring the wits out of everyone makes for a very practical application of one's time.'

'Can you not think of the possibilities of such a device?' Vey asked. Thordric thought he heard a hint of amusement in his voice. Despite Vey's standing as High Wizard, he rather liked to surprise people, particularly his uncle. Of course, being High Wizard also meant that the inspector couldn't say a word against him, no matter how much he wanted to.

'It takes a long while to send a message to stationhouses across the country, doesn't it?' Thordric said.

'Well, I suppose it does, yes,' the inspector agreed. 'But what does that have to do with it?'

They heard Vey laugh openly at this. 'Just imagine how fast the process would speed up if the constables at the other end could get the message instantly. To hear it directly from your lips, no less.'

'I must say,' Thordric's mother said, clapping her hands

together. 'That it sounds like a most intriguing idea. You said that my Thordric invented this device?'

'Indeed, Maggie,' Vey replied. 'As I've said many times before, he has an extraordinary amount of talent. Though his wits are not always as together as they could be.'

Thordric felt the blood flush to his face.

'Now then if that's all, Thordric, I'll be off to supper now. Don't stay out too long, you're leaving early tomorrow. Good-night, Maggie, goodnight, Inspector,' Vey said, and then the communicator fell silent.

The room was still for a moment. Thordric's mother and the inspector both stared at him.

'Leaving?' she asked. 'Leaving for where?'

'Neathin Valley,' he said, and then added quickly, 'I'll be boarding one of the floating Ships of Kal. You remember I always wanted to go on one, don't you?'

She narrowed her eyes and her usually bouncy hair seemed to curl into tight coils. Perhaps it was starting to behave like the inspector's moustache, Thordric thought, though he hoped not.

'There's a lot of strange rumours about Neathin Valley. They say that people have disappeared there, only to be found days later having no idea where they've been. I don't think you should go by yourself.'

'Nonsense, Maggie,' the inspector cut in. 'The boy's a grown man now, not the skinny green twig that walked into my station three years ago.'

'But what if something happens to him?' she argued.

'That's what the communicators are for,' Thordric broke in. 'I'll have one and Vey and Lizzie will have the other two. If I get into any trouble or find anything suspicious, I can call to them.'

His mother sighed. 'I suppose you have a good reason for going so far away. And no doubt High Wizard Vey supports it?'

Thordric shifted uneasily but inclined his head.

She sighed again. 'Then I have no choice but to let you go. But remember, if anything happens, I'll let Jimmson punish you for a month. And you must say goodbye to the twins before you go.'

Thordric inhaled sharply. His sisters adored him and he them, having them watch him leave would slice daggers into his heart.

'Alright,' he agreed after a moment. 'The ship sails at seven at the East Port. Meet me there and I'll say goodbye.'

'Excellent,' she replied, and got up to fetch her homemade carrot cake (which mostly consisted of grated carrot with a few crumbs here and there).

Thordric was so anxious that night that sleep just wouldn't come. Finally giving up and throwing off his covers, he got up to pack some more things into his bag. So far, he had three sets of Council robes, each of varying shades of blue, his underclothes, a generous amount of coins from the council treasury and a few books to pass the time.

He dived through his trunk to see if there was anything else he needed and found the velvet cloak Lizzie had given him when she had first trained him.

They'd been at her country house near Watchem Woods, and she had sent him out to study the plants and herbs growing there. It had been snowing at the time, so she'd given him her husband's old cloak, emblazoned with a silver half-moon.

It had been so long since he'd worn it that he'd almost forgotten he had it. He remembered what Lizzie had told him about the Wanderers. They were suspicious of members from the Wizard Council. Even though the symbol was different now, they would still recognise the old book and potion bottle from it.

Perhaps it would be wise to wear this cloak over his robes instead of his Council one.

He took it out of the trunk and, still in his night robes, put it on. It fit as well as it had before. Despite what the inspector said, he hadn't really grown that much over the years.

Smiling, he took it off and carefully folded it, placing it into his bag. He got back in bed and buried his head into his pillow.

A moment later he got up again, realising that he hadn't washed in two days. Throwing on some old robes, he grabbed a bright orange towel for himself and sped out of his room to the baths.

This late at night he had the room to himself. It had never been this quiet before, for he usually got there at the same time as everyone else and was the last to use the soap, which, by then, was frequently no more than a few flakes. Now, however, he found a full bar, placed there fresh for the morning.

The baths were large and set into the floor, so that many people could use them at once. Thordric had never really liked that idea, but it did mean that there were a few less arguments than there would normally be with such a rush of wizards in need of a good wash.

There was also a ceramic jar full of lavender oil, which he poured into the bath. If nothing else, it would definitely help him sleep.

And sleep he did, well until the sun came up. The housekeeper Vey had recently employed was far from amused when she found him sprawled out naked on the bathroom floor, with only the orange towel conserving his decency. He opened his eyes in time to see her flee from the room. He didn't think he'd ever seen anyone run so fast.

5

THE FLOATING SHIPS OF KAL

'Don't worry about it, Thordric,' Vey was saying as they made their way down to the East Port to find *The Jardine,* the floating ship that Thordric would be sailing on. 'She wasn't that shocked. I think it was more surprise at that bright orange towel than anything else.'

'I just can't believe it happened. To fall asleep in the bathroom with nothing on, I'll...I'll be the council fool from now on,' Thordric complained, catching his foot on a loose cobble and falling straight into a stack of luggage in front of him.

Vey watched as he picked himself up. 'Well, you do have your moments,' he agreed. 'But you shouldn't be thinking about that. You've got a long journey ahead; you'll need all your strength for that. Besides, by the time you come back, everyone will have forgotten.'

He smiled, his beard parting awkwardly down the middle, but it did little to cheer Thordric up.

They reached the ship; a tall vessel painted purple that was so large Thordric supposed it had taken several thousand trees purely to make the hull. Its masts stretched tall into the sky and, as Thordric watched, they unleashed the giant silver sails down to catch the wind. The whole ship floated ten metres above the air, with its mooring rope attached strongly to the docks. A long, steep ramp led up to it and he was about to get in line to board when he heard his mother's voice behind him.

'She is a very impressive ship, I admit,' she said, gazing at it.

The inspector was with her, and, to Thordric's extreme sadness, the twins were too. Vey saw them all together and decided it was best to give them a moment.

'I'll go and take your luggage to your cabin,' he said, nodding his greeting to the family.

They watched him as he levitated Thordric's bag above his head to make his way through the crowd. Usually, he would have had his guards with him; a group of high-level wizards who were skilled in defensive combat and magic; but as this wasn't an official visit and the fact that Vey couldn't stand them, he had decided to give them the slip for today.

'Doing rather well at being High Wizard,' the inspector murmured. 'Then again, he *is* my nephew, so it's no wonder he was destined for great things.'

Thordric didn't have it in him to snort this morning. The twins were already clinging to him, as though they knew he would be going away for a long time. 'Thordy,' they gurgled. 'Thordy stay to play?'

His upper lip started to tremble, but he refused to cry in front of the inspector.

'Not today, girls,' his mother answered them. 'Thordy has to go on the big boat. You've got to say goodbye to him now.'

'Thordy go?' Mae said, screwing up her face.

'No, Thordy stay,' Elle concluded. Mae agreed.

'Thordy stay and play today,' they both said and giggled happily.

Thordric thought of a way to explain it to them, but it was

no use. Instead, he gathered some rope that was lying nearby and fashioned them both a necklace out of it, attaching two gemstones that he had accidentally left in his pocket from an idea he'd had months ago, one for each.

Just then Vey came back. 'I'm sorry, Thordric, but the ship's about to sail. You've got to board her.'

Thordric stared at his feet, preparing himself. 'Well, I'll… I'll be going now,' he said to them all. 'Goodbye.'

He turned to go, but Vey caught him by the shoulder. 'Remember to test out the communication device when you get halfway. I want to make sure that it'll work once you arrive in Neathin Valley.'

'Don't worry, I won't forget,' he said, managing the slightest grin. Vey shook his hand and then watched him make his way up the gangway to the deck.

The floor beneath him creaked and groaned as they released the mooring ropes and rolled them up to sit by the anchor, which, Thordric saw, was gilded with the old mark of the Wizard Council, the book and potion mark, with a large 'J' underneath signifying it belonged to *The Jardine*.

The ship rose higher into the air, so high that he could barely make out the faces of Vey and the others below. Still, he waved heartily at them until the ship sailed beyond their sight.

He looked at his travel papers; his cabin was number seventeen, dubbed 'The Rookery'. He supposed he had better go and find it.

Making his way below deck, he was amazed at how large it was inside. Of course, it had looked large, but not *this* large. However, Thordric had found before that appearances could be very deceptive, particularly if it was something that Kalljard had been involved in.

The great corridor, which seemed to go off in several different directions all at once, was painted the same deep purple as the hull and silver framed paintings hung from the walls. Most of them, Thordric saw with disgust, were portraits of Kalljard himself. He supposed that Vey hadn't had the time to have them all removed yet.

Some of them, however, were of other members of the council. He thought he recognised the faces of some of the older wizards he knew, but most were unknown to him. He couldn't even tell which century they were from, for their robes were the same in every picture.

He shrugged and went left, after seeing a sign saying 'Cabins 1-20' pointing that way.

The corridor was slightly narrower than the main one, though he still thought he could comfortably have driven a cart through it.

He found 'The Rookery' easily and had barely unlocked the door when it swung open from the inside and a pale young man came running out, turning a violent shade of green. Pushing past Thordric, he rushed off in the direction of the bathrooms.

Puzzled, Thordric went inside the cabin. There were two beds in there, on opposite sides. His bag was on top of one, but the other had all manner of things around it. Books, clothes, strange brushes, and round pieces of glass for looking through (Thordric had never used one but Vey had told him that they made objects appear bigger so that you could study details more accurately) and, rather alarmingly, a pickaxe.

What kind of person owned such curious things?

The young man was certainly no wizard, for Thordric would have felt the magic in him. Curiously and, somewhat nervously, he picked up one of the books. It was titled 'Greatest Archaeological finds of the Century'. The other books were labelled similarly, a few appearing to be method books for various techniques.

The door opened again and Thordric jumped back to his own bed, hoping that the man wouldn't be suspicious. He walked in, seemingly unaware that Thordric was there at first, but then turned sharply.

'Oh,' he stammered. 'You must me my cabin mate. Sorry I ran out on you like that, but it seems my stomach won't settle now that we've started moving. My name's Hamlet.'

He extended a skinny hand and Thordric shook it. Now he was standing still, he could see that the young man was roughly the same age as him. 'I'm Thordric, part of the Wizard Council,' he replied, hoping that he didn't seem too pompous.

'Thordric? As in the Thordric who solved the case of Kalljard's death? I know all about you, you're a half-wizard, aren't you?' Hamlet blurted.

Thordric wasn't sure what to say. He hadn't realised that people would know who he was. 'Yes,' he said after a moment. 'I helped out in the case a bit. And it's true that I'm a half-wizard.'

Hamlet grinned. 'I always felt that half-wizards were more capable than everyone gave them credit for. You must know High Wizard Vey then? He's a half-wizard too, isn't he?' he gushed.

'He's a close friend,' Thordric said, 'and he's been teaching me since I joined the council.'

'Wow, you're actually being taught by him? That must be—'

Hamlet cut off abruptly, his face turning green again.

'Hold on a moment,' Thordric said, searching through his bag. He pulled out a small vial of liquid and handed it to him. 'Drink that, it should last for the whole voyage.'

Hamlet did as he was told and instantly his face turned back to its normal pale colour.

'Feel better?' Thordric asked. Hamlet gave him a weak, yet definite, smile. 'Good. So, where are you travelling to?'

'Neathin Valley,' Hamlet replied. 'My professor has some friends up there at a dig site and he wanted me to go there to get some field work experience.'

'What's at the dig site?' Thordric asked, starting to unpack his bag.

'I don't know, he wouldn't tell me.'

Thordric frowned. 'That sounds suspicious,' he said, looking at Hamlet directly.

'Not really,' Hamlet disagreed. 'He's like that sometimes. Though why he chose me of all people I don't understand. I'm hardly top of the class and I get travel sickness all the time.'

'Perhaps he thought you were more enthusiastic, or showed promise in some way,' Thordric suggested.

Hamlet made a face. 'If I'm honest, I think he just wanted to make mother happy. He's had his eye on her, you know, ever since Father died a few years ago. If he helps me get a job, then it'll make him look good.'

This made Thordric think back to when he'd first got a job at the stationhouse, working under the inspector as a runner. That'd only been because his mother had asked the inspector directly and he hadn't wanted to disappoint her. Though, Thordric had to admit, the inspector was a good man despite his bad temper and bushy moustache, so he had nothing to complain about. Unlike Hamlet, he had never known his father, so his mother getting married again hadn't been a problem.

Thordric looked at him as he thought this, taking in the well-kept blond hair and cream-coloured jacket and breeches. He was surprised to find that he felt sorry for him.

'I can't really do anything about your situation,' he said slowly. 'But I can help you with your travel sickness.'

He pulled out ten more vials and gave them to Hamlet. 'Each one lasts for three days. That should be long enough for me to do my business and get back to the council to make some more. After that, I can send you as much as you like.'

'Really? You would do that?' Hamlet said, blinking.

'Of course,' Thordric said. 'You won't have to pay for it either, because it isn't part of our product line yet.'

'But I must repay you in some way,' Hamlet insisted.

Thordric thought for a moment. 'Well,' he said, rubbing his chin and lamenting the loss of his beard from Elle and Mae's clutches the night before. He hadn't had breakfast yet and his stomach was throwing quite the tantrum. 'You could show me where the dining cabin is. I don't think I've ever been so hungry in my life.'

Hamlet laughed, a hint of colour touching his face. 'I suppose that now I feel better, I can eat too. Let's go, shall we?'

They left the cabin, locking the door behind them, and made their way back to the main corridor. The dining cabin was straight down the end, though it seemed to take forever to reach it. By then, Thordric was so hungry that he could have started eating the walls, but then the strong smell of roasted meat and vegetables hit him. He all but levitated himself after it.

The room was enormous and very busy. Thordric thought that there were at least a hundred passengers in there, but he was glad to see the serving area was still piled high with food. He and Hamlet eagerly set about pilling their plates with food of every colour, shape, and smell. It was wonderful.

6
INVISIBLE WALLS

'So, you say these wizards, the Wanderers, walked out on the council because they disliked the old policies that Kalljard enforced?' Hamlet asked, loading up his fork with ham and eggs.

'That's the sum of it, yes. I don't know much about them, but I thought they should know how much the council has changed. Even if they don't want to join, they should know that we don't pose any threat to them.'

'Were they threatened before then?' Hamlet said, shoving egg into his mouth.

'I'm not sure, but Kalljard was certainly keeping an eye on them.' Thordric took a sip of his blueberry and chocolate tea. 'I also thought of checking around to see if there were any half-wizards. See, like the old rumours said, if a half-wizard hasn't been trained, then his magic can go very wrong. Of course, the same thing happens with full wizards too, but most of them are found at an early age and put straight into the Wizard Council Training Facility.'

'But *you* used magic to solve that case,' Hamlet objected,

now helping himself to a large cheese puff. 'I thought you said High Wizard Vey didn't start training you until you had joined the council?'

Thordric smiled. 'He didn't, but his mother did.'

Hamlet dropped his pastry. 'You know a woman who can use magic?' he said, loud enough so that several people looked around.

'Not exactly,' Thordric replied, dropping his voice so that everyone went back to their meal. 'She learnt the theory from her husband, who was a half-wizard too and taught himself how to control his magic.'

'What happened to him?'

Thordric went silent for a moment. 'We suspect that Kalljard had him killed, though it's impossible to prove now that he's dead. I'm sure you're aware of the plans we uncovered during the investigation?'

Hamlet inclined his head. 'Everyone in Jard Town knows about it. He wanted all half-wizards eradicated, didn't he? I'm still not sure why, though.'

'He felt threatened by us. It's a lot rarer now for a full wizard to be born, as a lot of families are related to each other, and many have records of a wizard being born into the family. Kalljard knew that there would soon be more half-wizards than full ones and he also knew that when properly trained, there was no difference in magical ability between them. The myth that a full wizard has all the magic power that has been "stored" in the bloodline is nothing but superstition. Patrick, Vey's father, knew this and wanted to get back at Kalljard for all the hatred for half-wizards that he caused.'

Hamlet sat for a moment, watching Thordric finish his breakfast while everything he'd been told sank in. His mouth twisted into a wry smile. 'You suspect that the Wanderers are in Neathin Valley, don't you?'

'How did you know that?' Thordric asked.

'I didn't, but you unpacked all your belongings in the cabin. Only someone along for the whole journey would do that.'

Thordric smirked. Hamlet was certainly no fool.

They finished breakfast and made their way back to 'The Rookery'. Now that the ship was travelling at full speed, they could feel it rocking on the air currents.

Inside their cabin, Thordric got out his map to show Hamlet where he though the Wanderers were. Hamlet also got out the map that his professor had given him of the dig site he would be going to.

Laying them both out on the floor to compare them, Thordric noticed that the dig site was only a few miles from where the Wanderers were marked.

'It looks like you'll be quite close,' he said, tapping his map where Hamlet would be going.

'It's quite the coincidence, considering how large Neathin Valley is,' Hamlet agreed, marvelling at the detail on Thordric's map. It had been drawn by Kalljard, Vey had revealed, and he certainly had put a lot of artistic flair into it.

Thordric preferred Hamlet's map. It was accurate but simple and uncluttered by near lifelike depictions of trees, mountains, and rivers. It was easy to read and, to Thordric's amazement, didn't carry that strong musty smell that he had thought belonged to all maps and documents over a year old.

They rolled up the maps and put them away before sitting on their beds. The journey was three days long and they had only been aboard for three hours. What would they do now?

The creaking of the floorboards grew louder as the silence between them stretched. In the end, Thordric couldn't take it. 'I'm going up on deck for a while,' he said, and left the room.

As he reached the end of the main corridor, about to open the door leading to the deck, he heard a voice behind him.

'Wait,' Hamlet said, rushing up to him. Unfortunately for Thordric, it was too late.

He had already opened the door and walked up the steps onto the deck, straight into the cloud that the ship was passing through. Silently, he turned and came back down, his robes dripping with water and his hair stuck to his face. He saw Hamlet waiting with a towel for him and scowled.

'I did try to warn you,' Hamlet said, giving him the towel. 'After you left, I looked out the porthole and saw it was all grey outside.'

Thordric snatched it off him and busied himself with drying his hair.

'I wondered if you'd need one,' Hamlet continued, gesturing to the towel. 'I wasn't sure if you knew some sort of instant drying spell or something.'

Thordric scowled at him even more.

'How about we go to the viewing room?' Hamlet said, trying to change the subject before Thordric could get any angrier. 'I heard that it was finished with a special paint that makes the walls appear as though they're invisible. You can look outside even when it's raining or snowing and be completely comfortable.'

'I've never heard of anything like that on a floating Ship of Kal,' Thordric replied, frowning. Vey hadn't mentioned anything about it at all.

'The others don't have it,' Hamlet explained. 'Only *The Jardine* does. It's the best ship in the fleet.'

Forgetting that he was still wet, Thordric eagerly ran off in search of the viewing room. It was only when he found himself facing a crossroads in the corridors that he realised he had no idea where it was.

He looked around to see if Hamlet had been following him, but he was nowhere in sight. Nor was anyone else; the corridors were empty. Perhaps he should go back the way he came, but... which way was that?

It was no good. All the corridors looked exactly the same. He sank down against the wall, throwing the towel down beside him. As he did so, an idea struck him sharply in the head. The towel belonged to Hamlet; maybe he could use it to track him down.

Vey had taught him a simple location spell only a few weeks ago, though it had been to find objects, not people. However, Thordric was sure that if he tweaked it a little, he could use it to find Hamlet.

Picturing Hamlet in his mind, he willed the towel to go back to him. Within moments, he found himself being dragged along one of the corridors, turning this way and that, hitting all the corners and portraits as he passed.

The towel was speeding forwards as though it were being pulled by a giant magnet, with him still attached. Suddenly it stopped outside a door and threw him into it.

All too late, Thordric realised that it was the men's baths. He let go of the towel quickly but tripped and fell headlong into the deepest bath of the lot. At least the water was warm, unlike the cloud had been. He spotted a stack of towels, the same design as the one he had been holding, on shelves around the room. So, it hadn't been Hamlet's towel after all, he had taken it from here.

Slowly climbing out of the giant bath, he thought about trying a drying spell like Hamlet had suggested. Then he remembered it'd been a spell that got him into this mess and thought better of it.

After wringing out as much water from his robes as he

could; which turned out to be very little; he went back out into the corridor and bumped straight into Hamlet.

'Thordric, there you are, I've been looking for you...' he began, but then noticed the state Thordric was in. 'You seem to be even wetter than before. What happened?'

Grudgingly, Thordric told him. Hamlet laughed so hard that he gave himself hiccoughs. Thordric had no sympathy for him.

'Anyway,' Hamlet said, after he had recovered. 'I found the viewing room. It's right at the bow. You should see it, it's really amazing.'

A few hours later, once Thordric was dry again and his mood was less sour, he and Hamlet made their way to the viewing room.

Thordric blinked as he entered. It was as amazing as Hamlet had said, despite having seen plenty of unusual and magically advanced things at the council.

It was like being on deck, except that there was no danger of getting caught by the elements. The only way that he could tell he was still inside the ship was by looking very closely at the walls. If he did it for long enough, he could just make out the fine lines between the boards. Even the floor was transparent, which had made his stomach lurch at first.

'Look over there,' Hamlet said, pointing down and slightly to the left.

Thordric did. It was the tall peak of a mountain, covered with snow. 'Isn't that Mount Allja down there?' he asked in awe. They were up higher than a mountain.

Hamlet nodded. 'I studied it last semester. Did you know that they've found the bones of a giant bird there? There's no record of anything like it before.'

The rest of the day passed like this, with Hamlet pointing to every river, lake, and mountain they came across, explaining in great detail all the archaeological finds that he had read about and hoped to study one day. Fascinating as it had been at first, Thordric found himself dozing off against the wall.

Shaking himself, he straightened up, holding on to the wall for balance. As he did so, he realised that he could feel the magic from the paint flowing into his fingertips. Curiously, he felt along the lines of the boards and found that there were not one, but two layers of paint on it. One was the transparency illusion, but what was the other?

It was definitely a magical layer, but what it was for still eluded him. 'Hamlet,' he said, tapping his friend on the shoulder. 'Do you see anything unusual about this room?'

Hamlet laughed. 'You mean apart from the invisible floor and walls?' he said.

Thordric stared at him, unsure whether to be amazed or horrified. Why hadn't he noticed it before?

'What's wrong?' Hamlet asked, seeing the sudden change in his friend's expression.

Swallowing, Thordric said, 'Have a look at the others. Watch how they're speaking.'

Hamlet did so and let out a cry of alarm. At least, it would have been a cry if it had been aloud. He could hear everyone's conversations clearly, but what no one seemed to realise was that they weren't moving their lips.

'What's happening?' he asked desperately but let out another cry as he found that his lips weren't moving either.

'There's another layer of paint in here, doing something other than making the walls transparent,' Thordric explained. 'It's magic I've never seen before, so I'm not quite sure how it works, but it's allowing us to speak to each other with our minds without making us aware of it.'

Hamlet turned even paler than he was already and, with a bang, passed out on the floor. Thordric hadn't even had time to mention that the effects would wear off as soon as they left the room.

He restrained a smirk and dragged Hamlet out of the door and into the corridor. Absently levitating him back towards 'The Rookery', Thordric pulled out his communication device. He knew Vey had said to use it only when he was halfway on his journey, but the viewing room was so intriguing that he simply *had* to ask him about it.

Pressing the button on the small wooden box, away from where the blue flower poked out merrily, he called into it. 'Vey?'

He heard a sudden scrambling. 'Thordric? What's the matter; is something wrong?' Vey's voice sounded around him, slightly breathless.

'No, it's nothing like that,' he replied.

Vey let out a loud sigh. 'Good, you had me worried. I wasn't expecting you to contact me for another day. What is it?'

'It's about the viewing room onboard. Why didn't you tell me about the magic in there? It's amazing.'

Vey laughed. 'Well actually, I quite forgot about it. I'm afraid I can't tell you much though; the magic eludes even me. All I know is that the viewing room is the most recent addition to *The Jardine*. I believe Kalljard had it designed only a few months before he died. It was probably the last bit of serious magic he performed.'

7

THE WANDERERS

The *Jardine* pulled neatly into the docks of Neathin Valley, gently floating downwards until it was level with the ramp that would allow the passengers to disembark.

Thordric and Hamlet were up on deck, watching as the crew tied the mooring ropes securely in place. As the ship was still much higher up than most of the buildings Thordric had ever been in, he found he could see far off into the distance. He turned to Hamlet, who was also gazing out, a deep crease on his forehead. Thordric had never seen someone look so disappointed.

The landscape was completely flat, aside from the great drop to the valley floor itself, where he thought there might have been some sort of river flowing through in the past. Now, however, it was simply a giant dusty crack in the land, with hardly anything green or even living around it.

He wondered if there would be some sign of vegetation when he travelled further out to where the Wanderers were thought to be. There had to be something somewhere, else what did the people live on?

For as far as he could see, running alongside the edge of the valley, were groups of brightly painted houses in more shapes and sizes than he had thought possible for a house to be built in. It was as though a rainbow had collapsed on the whole town of Valley Edge, splashing it with a complete disarray of colour.

'Well,' Hamlet said, turning to him. The passengers were now allowed to disembark and, crowded as the deck was, they all began to walk down the ramp in an orderly line. 'I suppose this is where we part.'

He held out his hand, but as Thordric tried to take it, the sleeve of his robes slipped over his hand and Hamlet was forced to shake the fabric instead.

'If you have time, come and find me at the dig site,' Hamlet continued, now grinning. 'I'll be happy to show you around.'

Thordric winced inwardly as he thought of Hamlet talking to him for hours and hours about what he had unearthed there. Perhaps he could develop some sort of ear plug that would retain all the information within them so he could stop listening and just admire whatever it was by himself.

The thought made him smile. 'I'll definitely come along if I can,' he replied.

Picking up their bags, with Thordric and most of the other passengers staring at how much Hamlet had with him, they walked down the ramp to the docks.

A carriage was already waiting for Hamlet, so, after a last goodbye, Thordric watched as it pulled away, bouncing a little more than he thought was entirely safe. Hopefully, Hamlet had thought to take more travel sickness potion before he'd got in.

Thordric got out the pocket map that Vey had given him with the directions to the hotel he would be staying at inked onto it. The map seemed to highlight a single part of Valley Edge but, to Thordric's disappointment, it looked so like every other part that he couldn't even tell what direction it was in.

He turned and saw a man staring at him, so much the double of the inspector that Thordric had to stare at him for several seconds to make sure that it wasn't him. Even the moustache was the same, though he hoped it wasn't as responsive as the inspector's.

'You're from the Wizard Council, aren't you, young man?' the man asked, eyeing the crest on Thordric's robes.

Now Thordric was convinced. He'd pass out if the inspector ever referred to him as politely as 'young man'.

'Yes,' Thordric replied. 'I wondered if you might help me, sir.'

'What kind of man would I be if I refused to help a wizard of the council? Though, I must say that you appear awfully young. I heard their training took more than twenty years, but you look barely that age yourself.'

Thordric wasn't sure what to say. He could sense something, as though the man was a wizard, but it was so different to anything Thordric had ever felt before that he wasn't sure.

'I'm older than I look,' he lied, anxious to get to his hotel. This man, whoever he was, was beginning to make him feel uneasy. He held out the map to him. 'I'm looking for this area. My hotel is somewhere there.'

The man glanced at it. 'Ah, that's *La Ville*. It's quite a way out; you'll need a carriage to get there.'

As he mentioned it, a carriage pulled up beside him. He opened the door and gestured for Thordric to get in.

'Thank you, sir,' Thordric said as he climbed in, but when he turned around, he saw that the man had vanished. Shrugging, he gave the map to the driver and sat back as the carriage pulled away, bouncing and jolting as much as the one Hamlet had gone off in.

With his stomach starting to back flip, he desperately tried to find another vial of his travel sickness potion. He found one just in time, but it was half empty. Hoping that the dose would be enough, he gulped it down quickly, choking slightly as the carriage went over a particularly large cobblestone.

Strangely, he found that his eyelids were growing heavy. He must have drunk the last of the experimental batch which had sent him to sleep every time he'd taken it. A few moments later he was snoring loudly, startling the poor horse every now and then.

Instead of the sound of cobbles under the horse's hooves, Thordric awoke to a soft thumping, as though they were going along on dry mud.

Looking out the window, he saw they were. Instead of the bright pink, blue and green houses that they should have been travelling past, all he could see was a large rock, drawing closer by the moment.

'Where are we?' he shouted, hoping the driver would hear.

'Oh, you'll find out in a moment, laddie,' came the reply. Thordric didn't like his tone at all. What was going on?

His hotel couldn't be all the way out here; it looked nothing like the place on the map. He looked out at the rock again. That *was* familiar, but why?

Then it hit him, hard. He had seen that rock on Kalljard's map. It'd been in the area close to where the Wanderers were supposed to be.

The carriage stopped next to it and the driver got off. He placed a hand gently on the rock, which then flickered and disappeared. It had been nothing but an illusion. Now, where it had been, was a large hole in the ground.

Before he had time to wonder what was down there, Thordric felt something grasp him around the waist, and found he was being levitated out of the carriage and down into the hole.

He reached the bottom with a thump, and, with another thump, his bag landed on his head, knocking him out.

'Ah, you're awake,' someone said as Thordric groaned. The voice was familiar, but he couldn't yet place it.

He opened his eyes and immediately wished he hadn't.

The room seemed to be lit by the same floating fires as they had back at the council and, standing on the ceiling of the room with a few others was the person who had spoken. How was that possible?

Then, with a jolt that made his stomach jump up to his throat, he realised he was wrong. It wasn't that they were standing on the ceiling at all. He was the one on the ceiling, and they were looking up at him. Turning his head, he saw that he had been tied up with a silver-coloured rope.

'Do you like it?' the man said, and Thordric realised that it was the voice of the inspector's double, though his appearance had changed drastically. He was shorter now, with tanned, smooth skin and a coal black beard and hair. 'We call it a buoyancy rope.'

Thordric gave him a blank look. The man sighed. 'It's what's making you float up there,' he explained.

Still feeling the throb in his head where his bag had landed on him, Thordric said, 'Who...are you?'

The man smiled. 'While I was at the council, I was known as Wizard Tome. You can call me that if you wish.'

So, these people were the Wanderers. Lizzie had obviously been right about them. They were suspicious of the council.

'I bet you're wondering why we brought you here,' Tome said, a grin spreading across his face.

'Not really,' Thordric said. He knew his travel sickness potion had worn off, for apparently being on the ceiling for a long time made him feel just as ill. 'But could you bring me down now?'

He gagged, turning a nasty shade of green, and Tome realised what was wrong. Stepping aside hastily, he untied the rope and levitated Thordric to the ground, summoning a bucket from somewhere at the same time.

Thordric sat hugging it for a moment, waiting for his stomach to settle. Tome frowned at him. 'I thought you said you were from the Wizard Council?' he said, after a moment.

'I am,' Thordric said, gagging again.

'But you seem so...inexperienced,' Tome said at last. Thordric could see the disappointment on his face.

'I've only been there for three years. My name's Thordric.'

'Thordric? The name seems familiar.'

'I helped solve the case of Kalljard's death,' Thordric admitted, still cradling the bucket.

'That was you?' Tome said, sounding impressed. 'Then you really are as young as you look.'

He turned to the others behind him, and they all began talking in fast whispers. Thordric was still too ill to try and listen.

Eventually Tome turned around again. 'Wizard Thordric,' he said. 'We want to know why the council sent you to Neathin Valley.'

Thordric stared at them. He was starting to feel better, and, to his embarrassment, his stomach decided to growl loudly. 'Could I possibly have something to eat first?'

Tome growled as loudly as Thordric's stomach. 'No. This is an interrogation, not a social visit. Now answer.'

Thordric stood up, dusting off his robes. 'Vey didn't really send me here. I wanted to come to find you all myself.'

'Who is this Vey?' Tome asked.

'He's High Wizard. You didn't know?'

Tome looked down awkwardly. 'We were aware that there was a new High Wizard, but we didn't know who. So, this Vey replaced Kalljard, did he? What new absurd laws has he set down?'

'Well,' Thordric said. 'That's what I came here for. The Wizard Council has been completely reformed.'

Tome scoffed. 'As if we can believe that.'

'Would you believe it if I told you they're training half-wizards to become part of the council?' Thordric countered.

Tome raised his eyebrow. 'But half-wizards are dangerous, the council would never do that.'

Thordric rolled his eyes. He'd thought the Wanderers would be more open minded than that; in fact, he'd believed Kalljard's hatred towards half-wizards was one of the reasons why they had all left.

'Half-wizard magic and full wizard magic are of equal power when the wizard is trained properly. And if you don't believe me, I'll be happy to demonstrate for you.'

Without waiting for an answer, he levitated them all and stacked them one on top of the other, forming a human tower. Then he picked up the buoyancy rope and tied it around them tightly, watching them bob against the ceiling.

Thordric smirked as they struggled to undo it with their magic, but he was using one of the powerful bonding spells that Vey had taught him and, unless the person being held by it knew how it was cast, it was impossible to break.

'Now can I have something to eat?' he said.

Tome swallowed and gave a small nod.

8

SECRETS REVEALED

Two large platters of food were carried into the room by
the Wanderers and placed on the table in front of Thordric. Tome watched from where he was floating by the ceiling,
muttering curses as Thordric filled his plate so much that it
almost overflowed.

He hadn't trusted Tome to keep his promise about waiting
to question him until after he'd eaten, so, despite releasing the
others, he had left him up there. No one could do anything
about it, so he began to relax a little.

If he'd known that the Wanderers would be hostile enough
to kidnap him, he would never have dreamt about coming to
find them.

'I do hope you're enjoying your meal,' Tome said acidly as
Thordric took second helpings.

Thordric nodded, not trusting himself to speak with so
much food in his mouth.

'Perhaps you would be so kind as to let me down, then?'
Tome continued.

Thordric answered by turning him around so that his nose

was touching the ceiling. He swallowed and said, 'I told you, I'll tell you everything you want to know as soon as I've finished. Besides,' he added, thoughtfully scratching at the stubble that had started to grow again on his chin. 'Why did you disguise yourself as the inspector when you spoke to me at the docks?'

A muffled reply came from the ceiling, so Thordric gave in and turned him back around. 'What were you saying?' he asked, trying not to look too amused.

Tome scowled anyway. 'I said I simply happened to take on the appearance of a man I saw once while in Jard Town. He looked like the respectable sort, so I thought you would trust him. If I had known that you knew him, I wouldn't have done it.'

'He's my stepfather,' Thordric said, grinning. Then his smile faded. 'There was something else, too. I could feel you had power of some sort, but it felt strange. Like magic but not magic. Now you feel the same as all the other wizards I know, though.'

Tome snorted. 'You don't know much about us, do you boy?' he replied. 'We like to hide our magic in case there are any of you council folk about. Plus, the townspeople don't like us, considering how we abandoned it. It makes them think that we're untrustworthy.'

'You can hide your magical abilities from other wizards?'

'Of course we can, though why you noticed is beyond me.'

Thordric shrugged and pushed his plate away. He supposed he had better let Tome down; after all, he could have dessert while they were talking. Untying the rope, he levitated him down into a chair at the opposite end of the table.

'So,' Thordric said. 'What was it you wanted to know?'

Tome rubbed his bare arms where they had been bound by the rope. He wasn't as young as he pretended to be, and he bruised easily nowadays. Rubbing his face, he let his black hair turn back to its real, depressing white and his smooth cheeks became loose and weathered.

Thordric choked on his tea. Tome had been using magic for that long, while tied up as well? This was some powerful old wizard.

'Well,' he began, ignoring Thordric's stare. 'Let's start with what you *do* know about us. What's in your records?'

'Not much,' Thordric admitted. 'All we could find was a map telling us that you were somewhere around here and a list of names.'

'A list? Do you have it?'

Thordric reached inside his bag. He pulled out the note, slightly crumpled, and passed it to him. No sooner had he done so than Tome started laughing.

'This isn't a list of our names,' he said, his eyes watering with mirth.

'It's not? What is it then?' Thordric asked.

'This, boy,' he replied, 'is a list of all the wizards that Kalljard sent after us to bring us back. And there are sixteen of us here, far more than the seven on that list.'

'But what are the marks on the map for, then?' Thordric said, finding the map and showing it to Tome. Tome laughed even harder when he saw it.

'Those marks are where they must have been reported missing,' he said. 'We knew they were after us, you see, so we thought we'd give them the slip.'

'If they only lost you, then why were they reported missing?' Thordric asked, completely baffled.

'Well, we couldn't simply run away from them. They had ways of tracing us, you know. Instead, we used the Valley Flats to our advantage.'

Thordric waited, hoping for more of an explanation.

'You've heard of the disappearances around here, I

suppose? Well, there's a cave a few miles away that causes people to temporarily lose their memories. It doesn't usually work on wizards, but we found a way of increasing the power it had. After that, all we had to do was let them believe that the cave was our hide out.'

'But if you say the effect was temporary...' Thordric began.

'Ah, that was our fault. Because we'd increased the power so it would work on wizards, it also increased the effect it had on them,' Tome explained with a shrug.

'What happened to them after that?'

'They all found their way back to Valley Edge and settled down there. None of them had a clue what they'd been doing before; as far as I know, they're not even aware that they're wizards.' He looked at the map again. 'It seems you found us almost by accident.'

Thordric snorted. 'Found you? You kidnapped me, remember?'

'Ah, but you knew we were around here somewhere. Besides, it's lucky that we did kidnap you. You'd have found yourself wandering around near that cave otherwise.'

'You mean you left the enhancement spell on it?' Thordric said. 'What if a normal person went near it? They would lose their memory too.'

'Oh no, we'd never do anything like that. But we do post a guard there and, seeing as you're part of the council, he might have put it back on,' Tome said neutrally. It was Thordric's turn to scowl.

Dessert arrived then and, seeing as Tome took a generous helping too, they were left eating in silence.

Eating a large lump of ice cream far too quickly for his own good and suffering an instant headache as a result, Thordric realised what was really irritating him.

'How did you know I would be coming here?' he asked.

57

Tome swallowed. 'We didn't. I happened to be buying food at the dockside market when you turned up. I saw your robes and disguised myself to trick you.'

Thordric found he was disappointed. The Wanderers had turned out to be a lot less mysterious than he had hoped.

Tome put down his spoon with a decisive tap. 'Okay then, now I know that you're not here to track us or do anything funny, why don't you tell me about this reform you mentioned?' he asked.

'Wouldn't you prefer to ask High Wizard Vey about it? He's the one who's responsible for it, after all,' Thordric said through a mouthful of food.

'I would prefer not to travel such a distance for a simple explanation,' Tome said.

Thordric's lips slid into a grin. 'You don't have to.'

He took out the long-distance communicator and placed it on the table; the blue flower of the *Tenro Aqus* still poking happily out of the top. Thordric was rather glad that he had been watering it regularly. Pressing the button on the wooden box, he spoke into it.

'Vey? Vey, can you hear me?'

'Thordric?' Vey's voice sounded around the room. 'Where are you? Have you reached Neathin Valley yet?'

By this time, Tome had fallen off his chair. 'How...?' he began, heaving himself up.

'Who was that?' Vey asked curiously.

'His name's Wizard Tome. He's a Wanderer,' Thordric explained.

'You found them so quickly?'

'Well...not exactly,' Thordric said.

They explained to him what had happened, though Tome could hardly believe they were speaking to a man who was two thousand miles away. After that, it was Vey's turn to explain the changes he had made to the council; how he had stopped the hatred everyone had for half-wizards; switched to only developing useful spells and potions to sell to the people and providing magical support in case of an accident or emergency.

'What do you mean by "magical support"?' Tome asked. 'It sounds like a waste of magic to me.'

Vey laughed. 'You're not the only one with that opinion. I had a lot of trouble trying to convince some of our older members that it was a worthy cause.'

'Oh?' Thordric said. He'd been babysitting his sisters when Vey had introduced the idea.

'When there's a building that needs some repair because of a storm or other natural cause, we help to fix it. Actually,' Vey said, somewhat proudly, 'I went out to do some repairs myself last week.'

'I suppose I can see the use,' Tome conceded, though he didn't sound completely convinced. 'Since you claim the council has changed so much, do you expect us to come back?'

'That is up to you,' Vey said. 'If you wish to, then we will happily accept you back. If you do not, then we won't pursue the matter. Either way, the doors of the Wizard Council will always be open to you.'

'They're open to everyone now,' Thordric put in happily.

Tome stared. 'You're letting normal people see the secrets of the council?'

'We felt that it was best not to have any secrets,' Vey said, rather sternly. 'Secrets only make people suspicious and, after what Kalljard was planning, suspicion is the last thing we want.'

·   ·   ·

Thordric spent the night in the Wanderers' hide out. He found that it extended at least a mile underground and there were natural springs everywhere.

The hide out was made up of a series of caves, each linking to another and, Thordric realised, there was a spring in every other cave. Not only this, but the caves deeper in were covered in crystals and strange clumps of minerals. He even found a pale plant growing completely up one wall.

'Do any of these have properties useful for potions?' he asked one of the Wanderers, an ancient wizard named Yim.

Yim smiled. 'You're quite astute, boy,' he said. 'Yes, many of them do. That red stone there is what I use to colour my beard.'

He pointed to a large, spiked cluster of crystals that were growing just in front of them. Thordric saw that it was indeed the same colour as Yim's beard.

'Also, that vine over there,' Yim continued, pointing to the plant covering the wall, 'is particularly useful for making rope. It's what the buoyancy rope that we tied you with is made from, though we soak it in a potion made with certain minerals to increase its floating power. Without it, it only lifts you up by a few inches.'

Thordric ran his hand across it and found that his feet were starting to rise off the ground. 'It's amazing. Does it grow anywhere else?' he asked.

Yim shook his head. 'Many things in this cave only grow here. Even by the large springs, closer to Valley Edge, nothing like this grows.'

'Where do you make everything? Can you show me?'

Yim looked uncomfortable. 'I'm not sure if Tome would allow it. He's very sensitive about outsiders being here.'

'But he let me stay here,' Thordric pointed out.

'Only to keep an eye on you,' Tome's voice sounded behind him.

Thordric turned and found that Tome had once again used his magic to disguise himself. This time, he was a boy younger than Thordric, barely out of school. 'I'm going up to the surface,' he told Yim, ignoring Thordric's snort at how strange his deep voice sounded coming from the boy's lips. 'Keep him in your sight but let him go anywhere he wants as long as he stays down here. I don't want him going up to the surface and getting lost somewhere.'

Thordric scowled at him. Why would he want to go out in the dead of night in a strange place?'

9

TO VALLEY EDGE

Tome came back not long before dawn, or so Yim said and, after resting for a few hours, had agreed to take Thordric back to Valley Edge.

Feeling as though his muscles had turned to stone and his eyelids had frozen shut, Thordric found his way out of the room they'd given him and went back through the caves to where Tome was waiting.

This time he had chosen to disguise himself as the inspector again, though, Thordric noted wryly, he must have taken it from the inspector's appearance some years ago, as it was missing the great blossom of grey hairs that had started to appear recently.

Thordric was sure it was all his sisters' doing. He knew that when his mother wasn't around, the inspector had no control over them at all, even if he used the *Toddlers Instant Calming Powder* that Thordric's friend back at the council, Wizard Batsu, had spent years trying to perfect.

Tome raised his eyebrows as Thordric staggered towards him, hardly able to walk in a straight line. 'You seem far more tired than is natural for someone of your...youth,' he commented. Feeling groggy himself and with his back and legs aching, the word 'age' was something he wanted to avoid that morning.

Looking at Thordric properly, Tome frowned. 'Did Yim show you our Making room?'

Thordric tried to straighten up, but found it too hard. He gave a muted grunt which was all he could manage.

'And did he happen to give you some of the potion he's been developing?'

Thordric grunted again.

'I see,' said Tome. He let out a small chuckle, sounding very odd coming from the inspector's lips. 'I should have warned you. That particular potion has wonderful effects right after you take it, but in the morning...'

He reached in his pocket and produced a bottle of what looked like small chips of crystal. 'Here, hold one of these under your tongue for a few minutes. You'll start to feel much better.'

Thordric took some gladly, doing as Tome advised. Within moments, he felt so good that he could have raced through the entire hide out and back. He straightened up and felt the ache seep out of his muscles. 'Thanks, I'm not sure I could have gone anywhere feeling like that.'

They climbed up a steep set of stairs that led to a small opening directly underneath the hole that Thordric had been thrown down when he'd first arrived. He could see the illusion of the rock blocking the opening, but as soon as Tome touched it, it fell apart to reveal the sunlight from outside.

Compared to the soft glowing fires down in the caves, the light was so bright that Thordric had to wait for a moment while his eyes adjusted. As he did so, Tome levitated him up to the surface and then did the same for himself. It was even brighter outside than he had thought, for the sunlight reflected off the dry ground. It didn't make it any warmer though, for a chill wind was beating at them both.

'What is it you hope to find in Valley Edge? I thought your only job was to seek us out?' Tome said after swearing profusely due to catching his foot on a rock.

Thordric shook his head. 'That was only part of what I wanted to do. I'm hoping to find out if there are any half-wizards there.'

'Well, I've been around Valley Edge a lot, though I try to keep my distance from others as much as I can. I have felt a few inklings of magic now and then, so I suppose there could be some there. Of course, it might be those wizards from the council who tried to find us all those years ago. I never bothered to remember their faces, so I can't say either way.' He shrugged. 'What do you plan to do if you find any?'

'I wanted to send them back to Vey so he can enrol them at the Wizard Council Training Facility. He's a half-wizard too, by the way.'

Tome stopped to look at him. 'You know, boy, before I met you nothing ever surprised me. But now, everything you've told us is so different from how things were, I...' he hesitated, still not wishing to say the word. 'I feel as though I've *aged* more in one day than I have in my whole life.'

Thordric wasn't listening. 'When you kidnapped me, I was brought here in a carriage,' he mused, looking at the miles of dry landscape in front of him, with not even a hint of Valley Edge in sight. 'Why don't we have one now?'

Tome forgot his misery and looked rather guilty. 'We stole that one to bring you here; I had to return it last night. Bit of luck, really, swiping it. The driver had been answering a call of nature when my friend jumped into the driving seat. The horse didn't mind either, because we gave him a large bag of super oats before we got you.'

'No wonder the townspeople don't trust you,' Thordric murmured.

'What was that, boy?'

'Oh, nothing,' he lied. It appeared as though it was going to be a *long* walk, so they might as well have something to talk about.

'Why do you call yourselves the Wanderers?' he asked, watching as Tome strolled along playing with the inspector's moustache, humming happily. 'I thought it might be because you had no real place to stay, but if you've got a permanent hide out...'

Tome stopped humming. 'We don't call ourselves that, Kalljard did. If you really want to know, we call ourselves *Brothers of Truth.*'

Thordric sniggered. Tome rapped him rather sharply on the head. 'We were young when we chose the name and thought simply disregarding everything that Kalljard said was the true way to live.'

'So...you ran away?'

Tome rapped him on the head again. 'We didn't *run away*, we escaped from his twisted ways.'

'You still thought the same way about half-wizards as he did, though,' Thordric pointed out.

'We were nervous of them, I admit. After all, everyone has been told for hundreds of years about the dangers of them. I saw a lot of half-wizard magic go wrong with my own eyes, you know. It was just after I had enrolled at the Wizard Council Training Facility. I was only a boy, and like everyone else, never considered that it was because they hadn't been trained.'

'But that must have been a hundred years ago,' Thordric said seriously.

This time, Tome wasn't content with merely hitting him. Instead, he threw a handful of evil-smelling powder at his head that caused him to shuffle along the floor on his knees every few seconds.

'I may be old, but I'm not *that* old, boy,' Tome said and, to Thordric's horror, the inspector's moustache curled up to his nostrils exactly like the real inspector's did when he was angry.

'So why did you come out here, then?' Thordric asked, uncontrollably bending his knees to shuffle along the floor again.

'Because Kalljard had less control here. There's a lot of strange magic around these parts and he didn't trust it. That's why he founded Jard Town so far away.'

Thordric blinked. He'd forgotten Kalljard had been the first person to make settlements in what was now Jard Town. The founding of the Wizard Council had been his idea too, not long after Jard Town was built, over a thousand years ago. It was around then that all the hatred and fear against half-wizards had started.

He pulled a face. He, Vey and the rest of the council still had a lot of work to do in undoing everything that Kalljard had done wrong.

'What do you think the world would be like if Kalljard hadn't taken over everywhere?' he asked Tome.

'I have no idea, boy. There's no point in wasting time thinking about it either. No matter what you do, you can't change the past. Though I did hear a rumour once that Kalljard had been born sickly and weak, but somehow his mother managed to revive him. Gives you something to think about, doesn't it?'

. . .

It took them all day to reach Valley Edge, and a good part of the night too, thanks to Tome's shuffling powder. It was so strong that Thordric hadn't been able to shake the effects for hours.

They arrived, cold and hungry, outside the hotel that Thordric had supposed to have booked into on his arrival from *The Jardine*.

There was no sign of life coming from inside, nor any light. With disgust, Thordric spotted a notice on the door saying, 'Closed due to lack of business'.

What was he going to do now?

'You could always come back and stay with us, boy,' Tome suggested.

Thordric scowled at him. 'I'm not going back there unless you find a carriage.'

'Suit yourself,' he said and sidled off to leave Thordric standing on the hotel doorstep.

Throwing down his bag, Thordric sat down on the steps and huddled up against the door. He might as well get some sleep until the sun came up.

He woke to a sharp jab in his shoulder. Tome stood in front of him, twiddling the inspector's moustache again. Thordric stared. He hadn't expected him to come back.

'You found a carriage?' he asked, looking around to see where it was.

'No. I thought about what you said yesterday and decided that it wouldn't do you any good to stay with us if you want to find any half-wizards living here.'

Thordric looked confused. 'So, what are you doing back?'

'You could at least show me a little gratitude, boy. I've been wandering around all night for you.'

'Doing what?'

'Finding you a place to stay, of course. Now, get up and follow me.'

Grudgingly, Thordric did as he was told. Tome led him around the maze of brightly painted houses until he was so muddled, he would never have found his way out on his own.

'How much further is it?' he moaned. He found that his knees were all bruised, and it was all he could do to stand.

'Stop whining, we're almost there,' Tome snapped.

He was telling the truth, for around the next corner he stopped, changing his disguise from the inspector to a man who looked only slightly younger than Tome himself, though his hair and beard were a dull grey rather than white. They stood in front of a large house completely separate from those around it. As Tome knocked on the door, Thordric stared at it, for the house was almost the double of Lizzie's townhouse; the only difference was that it had been painted a vibrant orange with dark green splotches everywhere. He tried not to think of it as a mouldy-looking orange, but it didn't work.

The door opened and a woman, around the same age as Lizzie, stood there peering at them over her spectacles. She had red, frizzy hair streaked with grey and was wearing rather a lot of jewellery.

'Ah, Tome,' she said, inviting him in. She looked at Thordric, critically analysing his worn robes and noting the council's emblem on them. 'Is this the boy, then?

'It certainly is,' Tome said, and pulled Thordric inside.

Instead of Lizzie's tidy hallway, Thordric found himself squeezing past stacks of books, baskets and large wall hangings trying to get to the kitchen. He winced as he saw it, for there were plates stacked almost a metre high on every surface, not all of them clean.

'So,' she said, placing a rather chipped tea pot on the table and fetching some cups and a lopsided cake. 'You're the one Lizzie spoke of so fondly.'

'You know her?' Thordric asked, watching her pour the tea whilst spilling a great deal on the table.

'Of course I do. She's my sister-in-law. Eric, or *High Wizard Vey*, as he seems to like being called now, is my nephew.'

Now she'd said it, he thought he could see traces of Vey's features in her face – though he'd never looked as dotty as she was.

So this was who Tome had arranged for him to stay with?

10

MORWEENA

Thordric watched nervously as Lizzie's sister-in-law took a rather large knife and cut him and Tome a slice of cake.

'Well, you don't look like much, I must say,' she said, biting into her own slice and spilling the creamy filling all over her front, which fortunately she had covered with a napkin. 'But Lizzie seems to think you have some skills.'

She eyed him as she said it and then glanced around the room. Thordric looked around too and had a sinking feeling in his stomach.

Tome grinned at them both. 'I'll be off now. Thank you for the tea and cake, Morweena, it was delicious.' He got up, smiling broadly. 'I'm sure you'll both be very happy with the arrangement.'

As he disappeared back down the hall, Thordric turned to Morweena. 'What arrangement?'

'Tome said you would be happy to clean the whole house in exchange for staying here. And redecorate,' she added, indicating the peeling paint on the ceiling.

Thordric dropped his cake.

'Dear Lizzie told me all about the work you did for her, and that lovely mural you painted at her house in Watchem Woods. I can't wait to see what you'll paint for me.'

She giggled girlishly and cut another slice of cake, dropping crumbs all over the table.

Thordric sat watching her, unable to speak from a moment. 'I, er...of course I'd be happy to help,' he said eventually, forcing himself to smile. 'But I've got work of my own to do.'

'Of course, of course,' she said, waving her hand. 'There's no rush to get it all done, you can stay as long as you need. Perhaps you could try working on one room a day. I'm sure with your skills, it would only take you an hour for each one, so you'll have the rest of the day free.'

An hour? Even with magic, it would take at least half a day to clean it.

Morweena got up, upsetting the milk jug on the table. 'I had better show you to your room. I'm sure you'll want to get some rest after the trouble Tome told me about.'

Despite it now being midday, the house was dark inside and she led the way up the stairs by lantern light.

Thordric kept tripping up on things that had somehow found themselves stored on the steps. He didn't think he'd ever known anyone with so many things. How had Lizzie, who couldn't even stand a teaspoon out of place, have stayed in a house like this?

'Oh, she didn't,' Morweena said when he tentatively broached the subject. 'She's never been comfortable staying in the houses of others, so she stayed at the hotel instead.'

'But it's not open anymore,' Thordric pointed out.

'Yes, but it was when she was here. Actually, it closed down quite recently, a few days ago I believe. I know it says due to lack of business on the door, but there's a rumour going around that the guests there all disappeared.'

'And that's why it closed?' he asked, wondering if they had somehow stumbled upon the cave that Tome had told him about.

'Well, no one is certain, of course, but if it's true it *would* make the hotel look rather suspicious.'

'Who were the guests? What were they doing here?'

She stopped at the top of the stairs, frowning at him. 'You ask an awful lot of questions,' she said, but her voice was warm. 'I'm afraid I don't have any idea who they were. You should ask around the town, I'm sure someone will know.'

They came to a door painted vibrant pink and, as she opened it a loud clatter came from inside.

'What was that?' he asked, though she appeared not to have heard.

A moment later he found out. Like all of the other rooms, this one was piled high with books and, for some reason, a large collection of cooking pots. There was a small bed in the middle, but he could only get to it by clearing a path first.

'I'll call you down this evening for supper,' Morweena said, still somehow oblivious to the mess. 'Until then you should get some sleep.'

With that, she turned and shuffled out of the room, knocking a few books askew, and closed the door.

Summoning a flame like the ones that lit the halls of the council, he put his bag down on a clear square of floor he'd seen and sat on the bed. So far, his trip to Neathin Valley had gone anything but how he'd planned.

He thought of using the long-distance communicator to speak to Lizzie or Vey, but he wasn't sure what to tell them. Instead, he lay back and fell asleep.

'Boy? Boy, supper's ready.'

Thordric snapped his eyes open, but as he saw the clutter in the room it was all he could do not to close them again. Sighing, he got up and went down to the kitchen, summoning more flames to stop him stumbling down the stairs.

'There you are,' Morweena said, carrying a large soup bowl to the table. With disgust, he noticed that the milk and cake crumbs she'd spilt earlier had remained.

Without thinking, he used his magic to push it all into a floating, liquid ball and poured it down the sink.

'Was that still there?' Morweena asked. 'I must have forgotten to clean it. The soup's ready, by the way, so help yourself.'

Thordric rolled his eyes and sat down, hoping that she hadn't accidentally left any vegetable peel in it.

'By the way, boy, what is your name? Neither Tome nor Lizzie ever got around to telling me.'

'It's Thordric,' he said, lifting a spoonful of soup up to his eye level, cautiously analysing it before finally deciding it was safe.

Morweena laughed. 'What a curious name for a curious fellow,' she said.

Thordric felt affronted. 'How is it that you know Tome?' he asked, changing the subject.

'Oh, we go back a long way, do Tome and I. Very dependable man, you know. He was the one who decorated the outside of this house, not long after my dear brother left to marry Lizzie and live in Jard Town.' She sipped at her soup, managing to drip it all on her sleeve. 'Oh, bother that!'

Thordric cleaned it for her the same way he'd gotten rid of the milk.

'Thank you, Thordric. Now, what was I saying? Oh, yes, Tome. You must have been thrilled when he found you wandering alone so far away from Valley Edge. To think he brought you all the way back here, too. He never fails to amaze me,' she said, spilling her soup again.

Thordric spilt his too, though it was because he had snorted so violently that he'd made himself sneeze. So *that* was the story Tome had made up for her.

He supposed that revealing how he had kidnapped Thordric first would have resulted in lots of questions. Morweena clearly had no idea who Tome really was.

The next morning Thordric woke early. It had been hard getting to sleep in his cramped room, for the heat seemed to build up so much that he had to open a window, despite the heavy rain they'd had during the night.

Eyeing up the books and cooking pots, he resolved himself to cleaning this room first, else the next night would be the same. He supposed she had a loft room, so perhaps he could store everything in there.

'Of course I have a loft,' she said over breakfast. 'But I'm afraid you won't have any luck putting anything up there. That's full too.'

'But what am I supposed to do with everything?' he asked, noting a slight growl to his voice. Luckily, she hadn't noticed.

'Well, I...' she thought for a moment.

'Perhaps you could donate it to someone else?' he suggested.

'Donate? No, no, Thordric, I need it,' she said, laughing as if his suggestion had been a joke.

'All of it?'

'Of course. It's all terribly important.' She pulled at her frizzy hair, letting it ping back and then grasping it again, apparently lost in thought.

Thordric gave up and went back to his room.

He looked around it critically. There was no way he would be able to clean and decorate with everything lying around like that. He had to do something.

If he couldn't put it somewhere else or get rid of it, perhaps he could shrink it. That way, he would probably be able to fit everything into one box and, if he did it right, all Morweena would have to do to be able to read it at normal size was to pick it up. As soon as she was done, it would shrink again ready to be stored away.

Pleased with himself, he picked up one of the books. It was heavy and covered in dust, but he could just make out the title. *The Beginner's Guide to Cooking Pot Collecting.*

He snorted, making the dust fly into the air. At least it explained why she had so many pots dangling about. Sighing, he went through all the piles of books, gathering the dust and storing it within another floating ball. When he finished, he concentrated on making all the books smaller and smaller. It was harder than he'd thought it would be, for not only did he have to think about the pages getting smaller, but the words too.

To his amusement, he found that if he forgot to shrink the words in proportion to the rest of the book, they started to spill off the pages and onto the floor. Of course, when that happened, he had to spend time making sure that they went back onto the page in the right order, or else it became a jumble of nonsense.

He had barely finished fixing one when there was a knock on the door. Opening it, he found Morweena standing there with a tray of tea.

'My, what a clever idea,' she exclaimed, walking in, and staring at the coin sized books on the floor. Then she noticed the ball of dust that was still floating in the air. 'You know, I once heard a rumour that if you collect enough dust and push it all together, you can make some kind of precious stone.'

She looked at him expectantly.

Resigned, he tried putting pressure on the ball of dust. It resisted, sliding out of any gaps that it could find, but eventually he managed to squash it down until it formed one solid clump. Releasing his magic, he let it fall into his palm. Morweena was right; it had formed a pale green stone.

'I wonder what it's called,' he said, staring at it. Depending on the way he held it, it sparkled with a pearl-like sheen.

'It's called *Crystos Mentos*, I think,' Morweena said, also admiring it. 'It grows here, in the caves where the springs are. Many people believe it's what gives the water its power.'

'But I made it from dust,' Thordric said.

Morweena looked a little guilty. 'That's not normal dust,' she said. 'When I used to work at the springs, I took most of these books there to read. I often left them there accidentally, so when I brought them back when I retired, they were covered in cave dust.'

She picked up a book that he hadn't shrunk yet. 'Here, you might find this interesting.'

Thordric took it. It was a book about all the underground springs in Neathin Valley. He found that one of the pages was folded over and, as he read, realised that all the springs were linked to each other by caves like the ones in the Wanderers' hideout were. The only difference was that the caves where the Wanderers lived were deeper underground than the ones containing the other springs.

'Well, I guess I'll let you get on,' Morweena said. 'You keep hold of that crystal. It might help you grow a bit.'

Thordric fought hard to bite back a reply, contenting himself to drink the tea she had given him – but accidentally scalded himself instead.

11

FIXING THE APPLE CART

Despite what Morweena had said about Thordric cleaning and decorating a room each day, as soon as he was done shrinking the books in his room, she waved him off out the door so that he could go and explore the town.

He didn't complain; now was his chance to search for any half-wizards that might need his help and, the sooner he was able to do that, the sooner he could go home. It wasn't that he disliked Neathin Valley – had he gone there under normal circumstances, he would have found its strangely decorated houses and winding streets charming – but it was hard to appreciate it all when first he had been treated as a kind of criminal and now as a housekeeper and decorator.

Half suspicious that something else would happen, he tentatively stepped off Morweena's doorstep and into the street, which, for being just a side street, was curiously busy. Instead of wearing his Council robes, he'd decided to cover them with the velvet cloak Lizzie had given him. Although it still identified him as a wizard, it would look as if he were still in training and so nobody would bother with him. As much as he was proud to be part of the Wizard Council now that Vey had reformed it, he knew that if the people of the Valley Edge suspected who he was, he would be submitted to an endless stream of questions. Did he know High Wizard Vey personally? What really happened to Kalljard? How high up was he within the council?

Those were the most common questions all his fellow wizards had faced when they'd travelled. Everywhere, the people wanted to know what class of wizard they were, for supposedly, the higher up in the council they were, the more powerful their magic.

In fact, the class system had been another of Kalljard's inventions, a way of getting wizards who didn't always agree with him to behave by putting to them the chance of promotion if they worked hard and did what he said. There were three levels: low-level, middle-level, and high-level. Vey had been trying to eradicate them, for such a scale could never truly reflect a wizard's magical ability. However, many of the older members had fought against him, saying it provided a cause to keep learning and improving.

There had been a lot of anger when Thordric joined, not only was he a half-wizard, but the youngest person to join the council in history. Official training was hardly ever completed by a wizard under twenty-five, but Thordric, despite his efforts to grow facial hair, had clearly only been a boy of fifteen when Vey had introduced him three years ago. Not only this, but Vey had given him the title of 'High-Level Wizard' in order to teach him personally. No one had spoken to Thordric for weeks after that.

Sighing, he touched the stone around his neck that Morweena had let him keep. He wasn't sure exactly what had made him want to wear it, but it gave off a soothing aura and, for the first time since he had arrived in Neathin Valley, he realised he was happy. He also noticed that the bruises on his knees from Tome's kneeling powder had vanished as soon as he'd put it on.

He set off down the street, turning out of it and into what he hoped was a main street. There were crowds of people there and, Thordric found, they were as unusual as the houses looming behind them. He'd thought Morweena was eccentric, but apparently that was normal here.

A woman with yellow hair, done up in a high bun shaped like a banana and carrying a banana-shaped bag passed by him, as did a man wearing enormous pink sparkly shoes, so long that it looked as though his feet were at least three times average size. Another man and, to Thordric's amusement, a woman too, had grown extremely long beards and plaited them together.

Only one person was dressed normally, at least to Thordric's mind; a young girl with long blonde pigtails, clothed in a plain grey skirt and top with a leather apron over it. She was trying, rather desperately, to move a cart full of apples, but one of the wheels appeared to be stuck.

'Excuse me, miss,' Thordric said, braving the crowd to get to her. 'Would you like some help?'

'No. Go away,' she said, not even looking at him.

'But you look like you need it. At least let me take a look,' he said, ignoring her rudeness.

'I told you,' she said, turning around this time. Then she stopped. 'What funny clothes,' she remarked, staring at his robes.

Thordric laughed. After all the strange fashions he'd just seen, he thought he looked quite ordinary. 'I'm a wizard,' he said. 'I can fix your cart for you. It won't take long.'

'A wizard? But there aren't any wizards around here, they all live in Jard Town and that's miles away.'

'I'm here on holiday,' he lied.

She looked at him suspiciously. 'Go on then, fix my cart if you can. At least it'd be better than having my brother try to fix it with his crummy tricks—'

She stopped suddenly as if she'd said too much, but Thordric had heard her. 'What do you mean by that?' he asked. 'Does he have some kind of powers?'

'He only thinks he does. It's nothing; all he ever does is break things. Now, fix my cart and go away.'

Thordric looked at the wheel that was stuck. It had split slightly and gotten wedged between the cobblestones. Pulling it free with his magic, he fused it back into one piece. He moved it, testing it out. It worked perfectly.

'You really are a wizard,' the girl said.

'Of course,' he replied. 'If I push the cart for you, will you tell me more about your brother?'

'I suppose so. I'm going to the docks with it, do you know where that is?'

'Roughly,' he said, and gently guided against the cart with his magic. It rolled forwards at a good pace and they both walked behind it, following it up the road.

Most people didn't see how it was moving, but those who did hastily moved as far away from them as they could get.

'So, what do you want to know about him?' the girl asked, taking an apple from the cart, and biting into it.

'Well, what kind of things has he done? That have gone wrong, I mean.'

She snorted, making her pigtails flap around her ears. 'Almost everything. Mother and Father say that ever since he was little, he thought he had magical powers. I remember he tried to make Mother's expensive teapot fly once, but it crashed into the wall instead. He tried to fix it, but all it did was break into smaller pieces.'

Uneasiness spread down Thordric's spine. It sounded awfully like untrained magic to him. 'Where is your brother now?' he asked her, wheeling the cart around a sharp corner. Several more people scattered.

'I don't know exactly. All I remember is that he was talking about some discovery out in the Valley Flats a few miles outside of town.' She finished the apple she was eating and instantly reached for another one. Thordric wondered how she was going to have any left to sell by the time they got to the docks.

'What kind of discovery?'

She shrugged. 'I don't know, it was weeks ago. There was supposed to be a team going to investigate and he wanted to be part of it.'

Thordric stopped. That was similar to what Hamlet had been telling him onboard *The Jardine*. What if the dig site he was at was the place this girl's brother had been talking about? Perhaps he should go there after all.

They reached the docks a while later and, because she looked so small and plain next to all the colour of the town, he added a few things to the cart and expanded it slightly, cloning a few of the apples to fill the extra room.

'What's your name,' he asked when he was done.

'Lily,' she said, marvelling at the great silk banners he had put on it and the neat silver paint on the wheels. 'Are all wizards like you?'

Thordric smiled. 'No. Most of them are far more sensible than me, or so I'm told. Plus, the older ones get all grouchy and have long beards which catch all the crumbs they drop when they're eating.'

She giggled, but then turned serious. 'There's more, you know,' she said.

'More what?'

'More people like my brother. Mr Henders, from the hat

stall over there,' she said, pointing to a stall a few spaces down. 'I've heard that he can do things too. Or tries to. And then there's the drunken man.'

'The drunken man?' Thordric asked. It was unusual to hear of anyone being drunk, for as far as he knew, alcohol was banned throughout the country, for it didn't work well with any magic products. Nearly every household had some sort of magic product from the council; even here in Neathin Valley he'd noticed it, though it mostly seemed to be tea. In fact, there was a stall right next to them selling Thordric's favourite blend of blueberry and chocolate and a few others, each with a different healing property.

'I've never seen him,' Lily continued, taking another apple from her cart, and hiding behind one of the banners while she ate it. 'But Father says he wanders around during the night, drinking from the same bottle that never needs refilling. No one knows where he got it from anyway. Not even Shifty Tome sells it.'

'Tome?' Thordric said warily.

'*Shifty* Tome. He's another one, though I think he's different. Only us kids call him that, everyone else thinks he's perfectly respectable, but I've seen him stealing from people's carts and selling the goods to travellers as the Ships of Kal come in.'

So that was what Tome had really been doing when he'd seen Thordric. He hadn't been shopping at all, he had been stealing, like his friend had stolen that carriage. He wondered if Yim and the others knew about what Tome had really been up to. He wanted to think not, but then Yim's potion had had such a strange effect on him that it couldn't have been entirely proper either.

'What makes you think that this Shifty Tome is different?'

he asked. Yet again she had taken another apple, so he cloned a few more to fill the space that she'd made.

She thought for a moment. 'He does things, things he thinks people can't see,' she said. 'Like making things float over to him or making people look another way while he does something else. But it always works. I've never seen him have any accidents or break anything like the others.'

Thordric's opinion of Tome was sinking lower and lower. What a crook he was.

'I think he might really be like you, but he doesn't want people to know about it,' she continued.

Rude as she was, Lily obviously had a very sharp mind and her eyes caught even the smallest detail. She'd told him more in an hour than he'd hoped to have heard in a week.

He found he liked her, wondering if his sisters would be anything like her once they were older. 'Do you come to the market here every afternoon?' he asked.

'It's my job,' she said with a shrug. 'Mother works at the springs and Father is a sailor onboard *The Jardine*. He sailed out again yesterday.'

It was still early afternoon and, after saying goodbye to Lily, Thordric thought he would go and speak to the Mr Henders whom she'd pointed out to him.

He made his way over to the stall; a large purple table covered with ladies' hats. Surrounding it were two enormous treelike stands adorned with even more hats.

'Have you something you would like to buy for a lady friend, sir?' a small, hunched man asked behind the stall.

At first, Thordric presumed he was an old man, but as he looked, he saw Mr Henders could only have been in his late thirties, though his back was bent in a permanent stoop and his left hand was shrivelled and clawlike.

'Sir?' Mr Henders asked again.

Thordric swallowed. He could smell a nasty tang of magic coming from him. Magic that had gone horribly, horribly wrong.

12

HATS AND TREE BRANCHES

As Mr Henders was waiting patiently for Thordric to reply, he decided it would be rude not to buy anything. Perhaps Lizzie and his mother would like new hats, but which ones? He thought Lizzie would like something with flowers on it, but as he couldn't choose, Mr Henders asked him what she was like.

Thordric described her to him, mentioning her motherly, but sometimes schoolteacher like ways, and, to test his reaction, her knowledge of magic.

However, Mr Henders simply nodded and then brought out a hat so perfect for her that Thordric was amazed. It was a soft cream colour, decorated with miniature wax fruits and delicate blue roses and, placed between, was a small glass vial filled with a honeyed-gold potion that Thordric knew to be one of Vey's most recent works. Named 'Blossom Fingers', the potion protected the hands, feet, and other extremities from cold or extreme heat, and healed even deep cuts, leaving only a faint scar shaped like a cherry blossom.

'It's perfect,' Thordric said. As to how Mr Henders

acquired such a potion and how he'd known how useful it would be for Lizzie when she worked in her garden was a mystery.

'Mr Henders,' he began, as Mr Henders boxed the hat up. 'I was wondering—'

'Ah, but you wanted a hat for your mother as well, did you not?' Mr Henders said. 'Let's see.'

He looked at Thordric closely, peering over his glasses until Thordric felt quite uncomfortable.

'Ah, I think *this* would be best,' he said finally, going to one of the stands by his stall and taking off a red silk beret-style hat. Thordric blinked. It was such a good match for her that he could even picture her wearing it, the colour complimenting her silken brown curls and rouged lips.

Mr Henders *had* to be a wizard of some sort.

'That will be two hundred coins altogether, sir,' he said.

Thordric took out his coin purse and counted out the money in ten-piece coins. 'I'm sorry, Mr Henders, but I must ask you—'

'I know very well what you wish to ask me, sir, but I'm afraid I can't tell you here,' he said, dropping his voice. 'It's terribly bad for business, you see.'

'Then where would you suggest?' Thordric asked.

'You're staying at Morweena's, aren't you?' Mr Henders smiled. 'I live around the corner. Come over after supper and I'll tell you all about it.'

Morweena gave Thordric the directions to Mr Henders' house and, after supper as he had promised, he made his way there.

The house was painted a soft blue, much calmer than Morweena's orange and green. Before he had even knocked, Mr Henders opened the door for him.

Thordric went in and followed him into the lounge, where he saw a row of very neat shelves, displaying a large collection of hats. There was also a glass cabinet full of what looked like potions and powders of every kind the council had made.

'Ah, I see you've noticed my cabinet,' Mr Henders said, bringing in some tea. 'I've always been interested in magic. And yes, you are correct in your assumptions.'

Thordric protested that he hadn't been assuming anything.

'Don't worry, young sir, I'm not offended. This,' he said, gesturing to his withered hand, 'was indeed caused by magic. As you have also guessed, I am a half-wizard like yourself.'

'How did you know that?' Thordric asked, choking slightly on his tea.

Mr Henders smiled. 'Because you are Thordric, the youngest wizard of the council. You see, I was in Jard Town not long after you became a member. The entire town was awash with news about you, so I heard a great deal.'

'Then you must know of the council's reform,' Thordric said.

'Alas, I had left before High Wizard Vey had announced the changes he was to make, but my guess would be that he decreed all half-wizards be allowed the opportunity to train their magic and become part of the council too, am I correct?'

'Yes, that's one of the reasons why I'm in Neathin Valley. I wanted to make sure that all the half-wizards here know that they can train if they want to and, though I won't force anyone, I wanted to suggest that they do. Even if they don't want to join the council, because—'

'Untrained magic can be extraordinarily dangerous,' Mr Henders finished. 'I admire your concern, sir, but I fear it is too late for me.'

Thordric studied him for a moment. 'If that was to be

reversed,' he said, nodding to Mr Henders' hand and twisted back, 'would you reconsider?'

'If it were at all possible; yes. But even for a wizard of your skill I do not think you can succeed.'

'Well, I agree with you there,' Thordric said. 'But Vey could.'

'I would not wish to bother his reverence so,' Mr Henders said.

Thordric realised his problem. Mr Henders and, he suspected, most of the other people here, thought of Vey in the same way they had thought of Kalljard, like some sort of king or lord. But Vey simply wasn't like that; despite being High Wizard he still saw himself as just another person, of no more importance than anyone else. It seemed that only Thordric and Lizzie realised it. Even the rest of the council and Thordric's mother and the inspector regarded of Vey as a monarch.

'Mr Henders, Vey will help you if you want him to,' he said, pulling his long-distance communicator out of his pocket, careful not to damage any of the petals on the flower poking out of the top.

He pressed the button on the side and spoke into it. 'Vey, are you there? Vey?'

'Thordric, is that you?' Vey replied, again sounding as though he were in the room. 'I'm afraid you'll have to give me a moment, I've spilt stew all over my robes. I'll nip and change them.'

As Vey broke off, Thordric heard footsteps moving away and then the rustle of fabric. Mr Henders was calmly drinking his tea, though Thordric noticed his face was rather white.

'That's quite the device, sir,' he complimented Thordric.

Vey's footsteps sounded again, coming closer. 'Sorry, Thordric,' his voice came from the communicator. 'What was it you wanted to say?'

'Actually, I didn't call you for myself. My friend, Mr Henders, would like to talk with you. He's a half-wizard too, but he had a problem with his magic. He was wondering if you could help him,' Thordric said, giving the communicator to him so that he could speak into it.

'Your reverence,' Mr Henders began, but Vey interrupted him immediately.

'Please, call me Vey,' he said and then added quietly, '*I must do something about that silly term.*'

Thordric snorted into his cup.

Mr Henders looked uncertain. 'Vey,' he began again. 'I'm rather embarrassed to say, but despite everyone telling me to ignore my magic when I was younger, I took to practicing when no one was around. I...I injured myself because of it.'

Thordric broke in at this point. 'I don't think I'm powerful enough to help him, Vey. There's damage to his hand and spine and I don't know enough about anatomy to reverse it.'

'Well then, Mr Henders,' Vey said. 'Perhaps I can be of service. I'll book you passage to Jard Town as soon as I can if you wish it.'

Mr Henders dropped his teacup. 'You'll really help me?'

'Of course. Though I suggest you go through some basic training afterwards purely to be safe.'

Thordric returned to Morweena's late that night, for Mr Henders and Vey had spoken for a long time afterwards to arrange everything for his journey.

She appeared to have already gone to bed and so, feeling rather tired himself, Thordric did the same, glad that there were no longer any towers of books looming over him from beside the bed.

However, before he went to sleep, he picked up the book

she had given him about springs of the Valley Flats. There was a map inside, showing the locations of not only the ones open to visitors, but every spring discovered so far.

To his surprise, it even had the springs in the Wanderers hideout, though it said that the entrance had been blocked off due to the unsafe nature of the caves. Of course it was unsafe with a crook like Tome living there!

He shook his head at the thought, but then saw that there was a large spring near the location of Hamlet's dig site.

Not for the first time he wondered what they had found there, but he would still have plenty of time to visit after he'd found the mysterious drunken man that Lily had told him about.

Sighing, he closed the book and resolved to get a good night's sleep.

A frantic banging on his door woke him up. It was still dark, so he summoned a fire as he got up to open it.

'Morweena? What's the matter?' he said sleepily.

She was wearing her nightgown, with her hair frizzier than normal, and was shaking.

'It's terrible, Thordric. There's someone outside, he's trying to break in. He's using some kind of magic.'

'What?' he said, still dazed.

She didn't answer, but instead pulled him out of the room and down the stairs. Someone was shouting outside, and something kept on crashing against the doors and windows.

Wide awake now, Thordric pushed open the front door, but had to close it quickly as a large tree branch flew at his head. Morweena was right, whoever it was, they were using magic, for the branch had been too large for anyone to throw without it.

'Stay here,' he told her.

He opened the door again, this time ready to repel anything that was flying his way.

'You,' someone hissed in front of him.

Thordric summoned two more fires, lighting the street around them. A man stood a few feet in front of him, wobbling slightly. There was a bottle in his hand, made of swirled glass, and it was full of a brown liquid that he could smell even from where he stood. He guessed it was alcohol and, if so, then *this* was the drunken man.

'We don't need your help or your sympathy,' the drunken man spat, raining branches on Thordric's head.

Thordric waved his hand and the branches stacked neatly into a pile beside him. A whimper came from the man's left and, as Thordric enlarged the fires, he saw that Mr Henders was tied up to a tree with one of his own waxed fruits in his mouth.

'It's awfully rude to tie someone up,' Thordric said calmly, loosening the rope and removing the fruit from Mr Henders' mouth. 'Why don't you come inside and tell me what all this is about,' he continued.

As he spoke, the drunken man suddenly found himself tied up by the very rope he'd used on Mr Henders. Thordric levitated him upside down into the house, ignoring his cries, being extra careful to bang the man's head on the floor.

Helping Mr Henders inside, they all took a seat at Morweena's table. Still keeping the drunken man tied up, Thordric made him drink a potion he'd summoned from his bag. Within moments the man grew quiet and the harsh redness from his face had drained away.

'What was that, young sir?' Mr Henders asked curiously. There were marks on the man's arm and neck where the rope had cut into him. Thordric would have to make a poultice for him later.

'It's a potion to remove poison and reduce fevers. I thought it would help to calm him down a bit, though it might be a while before he's able to talk. Why don't you tell me what happened?' he asked, absently summoning one of Morweena's lopsided cakes to the table.

Mr Henders exhaled audibly. 'Though I hate to admit it, he's my twin brother. He never liked being told not to use his magic, so he went to live over in the mountains bordering the country. The people there keep to themselves, so he was free to use his magic as much as he wanted without anyone saying otherwise.'

'Why did he come back, then? Thordric asked, looking at the dreamy smile that was now on the drunken man's face.

'I do not know, sir,' Mr Henders replied. 'But he only arrived a few weeks ago, asking about a discovery further out by the springs.'

The drunken man giggled to himself and Thordric frowned.

He needed to visit that dig site.

13

THE DRUNKEN MAN

Morweena and Mr Henders quietly sipped the tea Thordric had made them while they watched him untie the drunken man. He put the rope on the table in front of him, a reminder that he could tie him back up again if he tried anything stupid.

Of course, Thordric didn't really need to tie him up if he did get rowdy; he could always levitate him up to the ceiling and leave him there for a while to cool off, but that wasn't usually the best way to get answers.

'So, what is your name? I can't keep on calling you the drunken man now that I've erased all the alcohol in your body,' Thordric said.

The man stopped grinning and sat up seriously. He frowned, flexing all the muscles in his body, looking confused. 'How did you do that?' he asked, his voice surprisingly soft.

'I gave you a potion,' Thordric said, raising his eyebrow. 'You were awake when I did it, it was minutes ago.'

'But nothing should have been able to make me sober. I

enhanced that drink so that no matter what anyone gave me or did to me, the alcohol wouldn't leave my body.'

By now he was shaking and, thinking the man was simply cold, Thordric gave him some tea and summoned a blanket to put around his shoulders.

'Why did you do that? Surely you didn't want to stay drunk?' Thordric pressed.

The man's eyes grew wide, and he shut them quickly, reaching for his tea. He shook even more.

Mr Henders got up and went over to him. 'What is it, Grale?' he asked, putting his hand on his brother's shoulder.

Grale looked up, directly at Thordric. 'The men who disappeared from the hotel. I know where they are.'

'Where?'

To his surprise, Grale summoned Thordric's map from upstairs. As it floated gently down onto the table, Grale studied it for a moment. Then he pointed to a single spot.

Thordric looked at it; it was Hamlet's dig site.

'They were working there,' Grale continued, pushing the map away. 'I came down from the mountains because I'd heard they'd found something that belonged to an ancient tribe; a tribe who also had magic.'

'What happened then?' Thordric asked. If the archaeologists were supposed to be at the dig site, why was everyone saying they'd disappeared? Perhaps they'd wanted to stay there for a few nights to finish up and hadn't returned yet.

Grale seemed to read his mind. 'I don't think they're ever coming back,' he said, withdrawing into the blanket. 'When I went there...' he closed his eyes, as though deep in thought.

Thordric waited for a moment, but then a loud snore came from Grale's lips.

'Mr Henders,' Thordric said, sighing, 'I don't think he'll say anything else tonight. We should all get some rest.' He stood up, promptly upsetting the milk jug, but he was too tired to worry.

Showing Mr Henders home while levitating Grale along behind him, he remembered that the girl, Lily, had told him her brother had gone to the dig site too. If something had happened to him, like the others, then he had to find out.

He hoped Hamlet was safe.

Thordric slept late, but Morweena slept even later.

To stop her from complaining and because he couldn't meet Lily until the afternoon, he continued to work on the house.

His room was now clear apart from the bed and, thanks to a good scrubbing, was clean too. All he had left to do was paint it.

She hadn't given him any specific colour scheme, so he decided to make the room as light as possible by turning it white. It had been a long time since he'd done any painting, though, of course, he didn't have to worry about paint or brush. Though he found he was quite rusty, long, graceful strokes of paint appeared on the walls as he guided his mind to each spot. The trick was not to lose focus, for a sudden stray thought could change the colour he was using in an instant.

Just as he'd finished, stepping back to admire his handiwork, Morweena came in and told him it was too white. 'A house is supposed to be filled with colour, not be without it,' she said, shaking her head.

He supposed it *was* a bit plain and the brightness of it reminded him slightly of his mother's morgue.

'I want you to paint every room in a different colour of the rainbow,' Morweena continued, tugging at her frizzy hair. 'Bold, bright colours, Thordric.'

She wandered back out and he sighed, starting to paint it a

rich blue instead. If he had to sleep in it, he wanted to wake up to a colour that wouldn't immediately give him a headache.

When he had finally finished, with Morweena's approval, he made a stop off at Mr Henders' house before going to the docks to meet Lily at the afternoon market.

'Come in, sir,' Mr Henders said as he arrived. Thordric noticed that there were pins, all with brightly coloured bobbles on the end, poking through his jacket.

'Did I call at the wrong time?' Thordric asked as he was led into the lounge again, where he saw that Mr Henders had been making some new hats.

'Not at all, sir,' Mr Henders replied, taking one of the pins and making a final adjustment to the hat he'd been working on. 'Grale is in the dining room. I'm afraid that he hasn't spoken a word since last night. I haven't seen him behave like this since our mother died.'

'Do you mind if I try to speak with him?' Thordric asked.

'No, please do so. I hope you can get more sense out of him today,' he replied. Thordric hoped so too.

He left Mr Henders to work on his hats and made his way into the dining room, where Grale was sitting with his back to the door and still wearing the blanket that Thordric had given him.

Thordric decided to sit opposite him, but Grale had his head bowed and so didn't appear to notice. He eased his chair forwards, trying to get Grale to see him, but he caught the hem of his robes and found his face propelled into the table. The crack of his now broken nose seemed to ring throughout the house.

Grale looked up at this and chuckled. Thordric tried to scowl, but his nose was bleeding and he had to quell it quickly.

'That's the trouble with you council wizards. You wear impractical clothes,' he said.

'It was a slight mishap. Our cloaks and robes are fine for everyday wear,' Thordric snapped, snapping his nose back in place at the same time. The pain vibrated through his body, but the bleeding seemed to be slowing now. 'Now, why did you attack Morweena's house last night? What's going on?'

Now that Grale was talking, Thordric didn't want to waste the opportunity.

Grale shrugged. 'I paid my brother a visit and he told me that the council now trained and accepted half-wizards and, even worse, the High Wizard was going to fix him up.'

'Why were you angry about that? It's all true,' Thordric said. Grale grumbled.

'We don't need your lot teaching us anything. I've been teaching myself for years and haven't come to any harm.'

'But your brother did.'

'That's because he wasn't determined enough. He was afraid of hurting other people, so he ended up hurting himself instead.'

Thordric fought hard not to protest, forcing his lips together.

'Besides, us half-wizards will never be as powerful as you lot. We're just not born with as much. You only want to train us to make you look better.'

'Mr Henders hasn't told you who I am, has he?' Thordric asked.

Grale shook his head. 'Why should he? Are you anyone special?'

Thordric smiled. 'I'm a half-wizard too. *And,*' he said, staring Grale in the eyes, 'I work directly under High Wizard Vey. He teaches me as well. Though I should call him High Half-Wizard Vey if you want to be technical.'

Grale swallowed. 'A half-wizard isn't powerful enough to

become High Wizard. This Vey you speak of must be lying to you.'

Thordric found he was angry. Not at Grale so much, but at Kalljard. If it hadn't been for him, all wizards would be seen as equal. He only hoped that Vey knew how many people still thought like this, though he was surprised to hear it coming from the lips of a fellow half-wizard.

'Vey is a half-wizard, like his father was. Ask Morweena, she's his aunt,' he said, trying to relax the tightness around his jaw. 'Half-wizard magic is no weaker if the wizard has been trained properly. Your magic may never go wrong, but it can't be very strong if you think all half-wizard magic is weak.'

Grale made to protest, but Thordric forced his mouth closed so that all that came out was a slight humming. 'Now,' he said, releasing him. 'Tell me what you saw at the dig site.'

Thordric ran down to the docks, hoping Lily was still there.

To his relief, she was, but he noticed that despite only having half a bucket of coins, her apples were almost gone.

'You're late,' she accused, staring at him coldly. 'You promised to help me move the cart again.'

Thordric couldn't remember making any such promise, but now was not the time to argue. If what Grale had told him was true, then he had no time.

'Please,' he panted, resting his hands on his knees. 'Lily, what do you know about the hotel?'

Lily twirled one of her pigtails. 'It closed about a week ago. I saw them put the notice up.'

'Do you know why it closed?' he asked.

'Yes, but no one likes to say it. It's because those archaeologist men didn't come back. Everyone thinks that they went out and lost their memory like the Strange Seven, except that they haven't found their way back.'

'Who are the Strange Seven?' he asked, though he thought he had a good idea.

'No one knows who they were before, but they wandered in from the Valley Flats with amnesia. It was a long time ago, before even Mother and Father were born, so they're all old men now.'

Thordric had been right. The Strange Seven must be the wizards that Kalljard sent after the Wanderers. If the people here simply thought the archaeologists had simply lost their memories and would end up coming back at some point, then that was why no one had shown any serious concern over it.

'Lily, didn't you say that your brother went up to a dig site?'

'Yes. He's probably got amnesia too, though mother says if he's that silly then he deserves it.'

'You're not concerned about him?' he asked.

Lily shook her head. 'I told you what he was like. It's probably his fault anyway.'

She peered at him, then back at her cart and the remaining crowd of people drifting away from the market. 'It's time to go. Mother will have supper on by now.' She started to walk off. 'Well? Aren't you going to help me home with my cart?'

Despite his panic over Hamlet and the other archaeologists at the dig site, he couldn't help but grin. He took down the banners and folded them neatly away in a compartment he had just thought to add and started moving the cart along with his magic.

Lily lived even further away from the docks than he'd thought, well past Morweena's house and that of Mr Henders, turning out to be opposite the hotel. So, this was why she had known so much.

He had barely finished helping her put the cart away in a

small, wooden shed next to her house when he saw Tome
strolling up, wearing the same disguise as when he'd introduced
Thordric to Morweena.

'Shifty Tome!' Lily said, standing protectively in front of
the shed.

'Don't worry, girl,' he said to her. 'I'm here to speak with the
boy, not steal your apples; though from what I've seen you don't
need any help with doing that.'

14

FINDING HAMLET

'I heard that someone attacked Morweena's house last night,' Tome said as he and Thordric left Lily's house and started back.

'Yes, someone did. I think you knew him as the drunken man,' he replied. 'He heard I was here to help all the half-wizards get training. He didn't like it very much.'

'So, he *was* a half-wizard then...' Tome said, scratching his chin. 'But where was he getting his alcohol from? To have a bottle that never needs filling is an easy trick for anyone, but magic like that always needs a base first.'

'Well, he did live up in the mountains, so he probably swindled some across the border from another country,' Thordric said. He stopped and looked at Tome seriously. 'There's something else, too. He said he came down from the mountains a few weeks back because he heard news of some discovery of an ancient tribe of magic users. When he got to the dig site, though...'

Tome stopped. They were right outside Morweena's door,

but that wasn't the reason. 'This dig site...is it the one a few miles from our hideout?'

'You know of it?' Thordric asked suspiciously.

'Yes. Yim went missing there.'

Morweena brought them both two steaming plates of meat and vegetables but, as she set them down on the table, she misjudged her strength and sent peas rolling about in every direction. Tome smiled warmly at her, but Thordric sighed and swept them all up with a small gesture of his hand.

'It's nice having a guest round for dinner, isn't it, Thordric?' she asked, as though he'd been living with her for decades. He grunted a reply and went to get the knives and forks that she had forgotten to put on the table. As he sat down, he saw that she and Tome were still mooning at each other, so wanting to eat his meal without gagging, he coughed loudly.

Morweena jumped as if suddenly remembering he was there and turned to him. 'Oh yes,' she said. 'What is all this mysterious talk about that dig site out in the Valley Flats? What's going on there?'

'That's what I'm going to find out,' said Thordric, stabbing mercilessly at his meat.

She watched him for a moment and then looked at Tome for an explanation.

Tome cleared his throat impressively. 'Those guests staying at the hotel disappeared there, as did one of my friends and, we think, a young boy from around here. Thordric's friend also left for the dig site the same day he arrived here, but—'

'I haven't heard any news of him, so I'm not even certain if he got there,' Thordric interrupted, taking a great gulp of tea. 'And you still haven't told me what Yim was doing there.'

'Oh yes,' Tome said, scratching at the short grey beard of his disguise. He pushed his plate back and folded his arms across the table in thought. 'Last thing I heard, he went out for supplies for his, er, project,' he said, looking awkwardly at Morweena.

She swooned back at him, her hands clasped together by her face with her elbows resting in the gravy boat, having no idea he was talking about the potion that had made Thordric so ill the morning after he'd taken it.

'Some of the things he needed were located by that special cave I told you about, boy. As it turns out, it's not very far from where the dig site is and, being the curious sort, Yim went to investigate. He didn't come back, so I was called out to have a look, but when I arrived, there was no dig site at all. It looked like some strange jungle or forest had sprouted in the middle of the Valley Flats. It had such a strange feel to it that I didn't want to get too close.'

Thordric put his fork down. Tome's story matched with what Grale had told him. 'I'm going there tomorrow. I have to.'

'Well, that's your choice, boy. But I'd be careful around there,' Tome said.

'You should go with him, Tome. A young man like him might need the help of someone dependable,' Morweena said, leaning in towards him.

Thordric thought he might be sick. Even Tome looked uncomfortable.

'Now, now, Morweena, he's a wizard from the council. I'm simply a humble old man trying to keep active,' he said.

Thordric snorted, but Morweena scoffed at the same time. 'What if he finds his friend injured over there? How would he carry him back?'

Had she not been watching every time he'd levitated something? And, more to the point, how could she trust such a crook as Tome?

'Alright,' Tome gave in, squirming under her goggle-eyed stare. 'I'll go with him.'

The next morning, Tome somehow managed to procure a carriage without payment. As long as they got there, Thordric thought it best to ignore such an illegal act. After all, his money purse was feeling rather light after he had bought those hats for Lizzie and his mother.

Once again, he had decided to wear his *Crystos Mentos* around his neck, for if the situation was as bad as he thought, he would need his head calm enough to think properly. Due to the heat, he'd also decided to forego his cloak and wear just his robes instead.

Like the last carriage, this one bounced about so much that he started feeling ill again, but this time he had no potion left to take it away. Instead, Tome threw another kind of powder in his face, which, though it took his travel sickness away, now made Thordric sneeze every few minutes instead.

'Even magic is no cure-all, boy,' Tome said rather cheerfully. Thordric thought the old wizard was rather enjoying the situation.

After a few hours, they stopped. As Thordric stumbled out of the carriage, he saw Tome loosen the harness on the horse's back and summon it a large bucket of water and a bag of super oats, patting its neck affectionately.

So, Tome wasn't that bad after all.

'Where is it, then?' Thordric asked, looking around for the dig site.

Tome pointed behind him. Thordric turned.

A wall of giant trees was sprouting out of the ground perhaps half a mile away and, as Thordric looked closer, there seemed to be more sprouting up. They were growing from small saplings into great giants in a matter of minutes and were spreading further and further out.

'I didn't want to take the carriage too close,' Tome said, still patting the horse.

Thordric understood why. Even from this distance it was disturbing and, if the horse bolted, they would be stuck there on foot.

'Let's go, then,' he said, trying not to think about what he might find there.

They made their way over to the trees, with more still growing by the minute. The rest of the Valley Flats were still dusty and barren. It didn't make sense; not even a powerful spell could make that many trees grow in a place that wasn't fertile.

The closer they got, the more Tome complained that they should head back. He said there was a strange feel to the air that wasn't like any magic he had ever felt before. Thordric felt it too, but for some reason it compelled him to carry on instead of turning away.

'I don't like this, boy,' Tome said, stopping as they reached the first few trees. 'I have this strange feeling in my bones, like they're stiffening somehow.'

Thordric grunted and pushed Tome further in. 'It's purely your age,' he said.

'Nonsense, boy, my body is in fine condition. I'm telling you it's something to do with all these trees.'

It was dark among the trees, so Thordric tried to summon a fire, but for some reason it wouldn't come. Frowning, he rummaged around in his bag and produced a small globe with liquid inside. He shook it and it lit up, relieving some of the gloom for them.

'Here,' he said to Tome, and gave him one too. Now with

the light from both globes, they could just make out the ground, covered in giant roots and creeping plants.

They went deeper in, where the trees grew closer together and there was no clear path through them. A loud cracking sound came from in front of them and they saw some of the smaller plants move. Thordric went forwards slowly, but somehow, he caught his foot in a root on the ground and ended up with his face in the dirt.

He sat up, checking that he hadn't broken his nose again and saw that it hadn't been a tree root that had made him fall at all. It was the strap of a large, leather bag. 'Tome, lift your globe higher,' he said, bending over the bag. Inside it were tools similar to the ones Hamlet'd had. 'Tome, what do you think...'

But he stopped, looking around. Tome had vanished.

In his place, with the globe resting between its branches, was another tree. That was odd; Tome wouldn't have gone without saying anything...surely?

However, as Thordric looked closer, he couldn't help but cry out in horror. He stumbled back over the bag again, falling to the ground once more.

The tree was shaped like a man, with a gap in its trunk to make up the legs and two thick branches at the top, one curiously growing down, the other held out with the globe balanced on it, as though lighting the way. Growing from the two arm branches was a thinner one that then bulged out into an oblong shape, like a neck and head. Long spindly branches grew from the top like hair and, where a chin would be, some kind of lichen had grown to form a beard.

Thordric could only come to one conclusion. Tome had turned into this strange tree.

There was another loud snap, making him jump up against the tree, knocking the light globe from the branch. He heard someone behind him and turned in time to see that whoever it was had picked the globe up and was holding it out to him, hiding their face.

He took it, his arm shaking, but then drew in a breath. 'Hamlet?'

'So, it is you, Thordric,' Hamlet said, his eyes shut. 'I've been in the dark so long that I'm afraid that light is too bright for me.'

Thordric put the globe away hastily, picking up his own one and putting a dimming spell on it. The light shrank back to a soft, pale glow that only let him see Hamlet's face. His pale skin was covered with dirty smudges and there was a large scratch above his eye.

'What happened here?' Thordric said, still staring at him.

'I'll tell you when we get closer to the main excavation area. It's this way.' Hamlet turned, taking the sleeve of Thordric's robes, and led him deeper into the forest. 'Don't worry,' he added. 'If you've made it this far then nothing will happen to you.'

Despite being reassured, Thordric felt rather weak. Still, he let Hamlet pull him through the trees, hoping that he would explain all of this.

Some of the trees had fallen over, meaning they had to climb over them. Here and there, Thordric saw more equipment scattered about on the floor. At one point, when Hamlet paused to let Thordric catch his breath, he could have sworn veins of gold were running through the ground.

When they finally reached the place where Hamlet wanted to stop, Thordric found that they were in a small clearing, hardly big enough for the tent that had been set up there. Unzipping the opening, Hamlet went inside. Thordric followed.

'Tea?' Hamlet asked, propping up a miniature cooking stove and a kettle.

'Yes, please,' Thordric heard himself saying, despite thinking that this was hardly the time for it. He looked around nervously, peering out of the tent flap every few moments.

'The trees won't grow in this area. I'm not sure why, but they don't seem to like it. That's why I kept the tent here.'

He poured the tea and gave it to Thordric. Thordric took a long drink, noting that it was one of the newest brews Wizard Myak had developed. Unfortunately, it was one for alertness, so far from calming him down it made him worse.

'Sorry,' Hamlet said, watching as Thordric's eyes bulged slightly and he twitched now and then. 'It's the only tea I have left. I had to use all of the calming ones myself.'

15

TREES, TREES, TREES!

'The trees had already started growing when I arrived,' Hamlet said. 'They extended out perhaps half as far as they do now. At first, I thought they were supposed to be here, but they covered the entire dig site and there was no one around. It seems the more days that pass, the faster they grow.'

Thordric watched him, feeling the tea losing its effect finally, though it should have lasted much longer than that. Hamlet suddenly pointed to the *Crystos Mentos* around Thordric's neck; it was glowing faintly. 'I've never seen a stone glow like that before,' he commented.

Was that what was taking away the effects of the tea so quickly?

'Anyway,' Hamlet continued, shifting slightly. 'I thought that maybe they had gone back to their hotel in Valley Edge, and I thought about going there too, but my professor didn't give me enough funds to stay anywhere except this tent.

'I found my way by following those veins of gold that I believe you saw on the floor. They all lead here, you know. Once I got here, I found they'd left a lot of equipment behind, some of it so delicate that it might have been ruined had I not taken it down and put it away. That's when I noticed them. Five oddly shaped trees, all in the centre of this place. One even looks as though it's dusting off an artefact, but the roots everywhere seem to have completely covered whatever it was.'

'Are they still there?' Thordric asked, trying to crane his neck under the tent flap but falling off his chair instead.

Hamlet laughed quietly. 'You can't see them from here, there's a thorn bush of some sort hiding them. That's how I got this scratch,' he said, indicating the one above his eye.

Thordric rubbed his chin, disappointed, and sat back up. 'You think those trees were once human, like Tome?'

'Your friend back there? Yes, I do. Particularly after what I saw the day before yesterday.'

'Oh?' Thordric prompted.

'I was out near to where I found you just now, looking for some clue as to what caused all of this. Someone was walking around in here, so I went to see who it was. There was an old man rummaging around the tree roots. He had a curiously red beard but a head of white hair...You know him?' he asked, seeing the horror on Thordric's face.

'Yes; at least I think I do. He's a wizard named Yim. One of the Wanderers I told you about on *The Jardine*. Tome was one too.'

'Well, that puts my theory to bed,' Hamlet said, put out.

'Theory?'

'I thought when I saw you here that wizards might be free from this thing, but if you say that old man was one, then I must be wrong. I watched him turn into a tree. It was like he'd been frozen, but then his skin, even his clothes, turned into wood along with his features. The only way you could tell it had been him at all was by the beard of lichen covering it.'

Thordric chewed his lip. Grale had told him the truth after

all; he'd seen the missing men turn into trees. It was enough to make anyone want to forget it.

He stood up to stretch his legs, his hair brushing against the top of the tent. 'So, you still don't know what this big discovery was that you were sent here to dig up?' he asked.

'No,' Hamlet said, shaking his head. 'The roots growing over it can't be cut. They can't even be burnt.'

'I think you should take me there,' Thordric said.

Hamlet agreed and led him back out of the tent. Behind it, as he'd said, was a thorn bush growing at least six feet high, though there was a small hole in it which looked as though someone had squeezed through.

Hamlet went through it, holding his arms over his face. Thordric did the same, but there was a long tearing sound as his robes caught the thorns. He looked down and found there was now a large slit going up to his hip, revealing part of his under-clothes. Blushing slightly, he tried to fix it. What should have been an easy spell took him almost five minutes, for his magic still didn't want to come.

'Here they are,' Hamlet said in front of him. Thordric hoped he hadn't noticed anything.

He looked to where Hamlet was pointing. There were five trees, all looking eerily human. Examining the closest one, Thordric found there was a pickaxe embedded in it, though it was the handle that was attached to it instead of the axe head, as if the tree was holding it. Another appeared to be clutching a lamp and, looking at the one Hamlet had said was crouching down, he saw various brushes and scraping tools embedded in the roots by its feet and one in its hand.

In the middle of them, for they all appeared to be crowding around one point, was a mass of roots all growing into each other forming a mound. The strange feeling that he and Tome had felt was strongest at this point. He had no doubt that whatever was causing all of this was emanating from there.

'Hamlet,' he asked, getting closer to the mound. 'Do you feel anything strange here?'

Hamlet turned from where he stood examining a vein of gold that was visible through the roots. 'Like what?' he asked.

That confirmed it. This feeling, though it was very different from what he was used to, was definitely some kind of magic. Perhaps it was the magic of the ancient tribe and, in trying to dig it up, the archaeologists had disturbed it and released it into the ground.

But why was it that neither he nor Hamlet had turned into trees?

'I'm going to try and cut away those roots,' he said finally, after thinking about it for a few minutes. Maybe it would respond to a magical axe.

He thought about the sharpness of a real axe, able to cut through even the toughest of woods, and willed that sharpness to slice through the roots. A cut appeared in the top root, so he chopped at it again and another cut appeared, but as he turned to tell Hamlet, he saw that the cuts simply vanished.

Frowning, he tried it again, faster this time, but the faster he chopped the faster the roots healed. They were impenetrable.

Giving up, he sat on the ground with a thump.

A sapling grew up beside him and then another and another. In moments he was surrounded, and the trees were maturing fast. If he stayed where he was, he would be trapped by them, or worse. He sprang up out of the way, breathing heavily as he saw he'd made it in time. The trees closed together until they formed one giant trunk; if he had stayed between them, he would have been crushed.

'Hamlet,' he said, grabbing the pale young man by the arm. 'We're leaving.'

Pulling him back through the trees, he didn't stop until they were free of them, outside in the sunlight. To his surprise, he found that they were only a few metres away from the carriage and the horse was staring at them wildly and thrashing about in its loosened harness.

The trees were growing even faster now and had taken up almost half a mile more in the few hours that Thordric had been in there. At this rate it would reach Valley Edge in a few days, and he thought the trees were unlikely to stop in the presence of houses.

In the carriage he found some more super oats and a packet of one of Tome's powders. It was labelled 'Steady heart', and, hoping desperately that it would calm the poor horse down enough to take them away from here, he sprinkled some of it onto the super oats.

He ordered Hamlet to stay in the carriage while he gave the oats to the horse, patting it soothingly as Tome had done. He could feel its racing pulse slowing down to normal speed and, with the back of his sleeve, he wiped the foam away from its mouth. The powder was working and in a few moments the horse was still enough for Thordric to retighten the harness and hop up to the driver's seat.

Taking the reins and clicking his tongue as he'd seen Tome do, he urged the horse to move. It looked at him for a moment, unsure at having such an inexperienced driver, but seemed to decide that the situation was too urgent to worry and so turned the carriage around in the direction of Valley Edge.

The ride was bumpy, but neither he nor Hamlet were calm enough to be troubled by their usual travel sickness. By late afternoon, aching and bruised and with sweat dripping off the horse's back like raindrops, they finally reached Morweena's house.

Having no idea where Tome had got the carriage from, he

left it in front of the house and took the horse around to the back where he quickly put together a stable in her garden. Once the horse was settled, he and Hamlet went inside.

'Goodness, Thordric,' she said, coming out of the lounge with her jewellery clinking together noisily. 'Whatever happened to you? And where's Tome? Why isn't he with you?'

Thordric led her slowly into the kitchen, telling Hamlet to follow. He sat her down at the table and then fetched the kettle and some cake.

Morweena glanced from him to Hamlet, a look of panic on her face. Thordric realised then that both he and Hamlet were bleeding from running back through the trees. He summoned some bandages and put them on the table, telling Hamlet to roll up his sleeves so that he could clean his cuts and apply the all-purpose salve that Lizzie had given him a few months before.

Once the tea was ready and their wounds had all been bound, he decided he had put off telling Morweena what happened for long enough.

With Hamlet's help he explained everything, starting with when he and Tome had first entered the forest and felt something strange there. She let out a whimper when he told her what had happened to him and, forgetting that she hadn't known who Tome really was, he told her of how it had ruined Hamlet's theory of only wizards being able to withstand it.

It was then that Thordric noticed that even if it had been right, it didn't explain why Hamlet himself was fine, for he still could not sense any magic about him.

Thordric studied him. There were still smudges of dirt on his face and his blond hair was caked in mud and leaves. Then, sticking out the top of his torn shirt, Thordric saw a silver chain around his neck. 'What's that?' he asked curiously.

Hamlet blinked. 'Hmm? Oh, this?' he said, pulling the chain out to reveal a small bottle of pale green crystals. 'My father gave these to me before he died. He said they had been in his family for generations and that they would protect me if I ever got into trouble.'

'May I?' Thordric asked.

Hamlet offered the bottle to him. Thordric opened it gently and took one of the tiny stones out. It was the same as his *Crystos Mentos*, though it felt much, much, older. He put it back in the bottle and gave it back to Hamlet.

'I think I know why we didn't turn into trees. It's these stones,' he said. 'I might be wrong, but I think they directed that odd magic away from us. Remember when mine was glowing after you gave me that tea?'

Hamlet nodded.

'I'm sure it was weakening the effect because it wasn't what I needed right then. If it can do that, then perhaps it can weaken the effect of other magic too.'

'Is that what was making it hard for you to use your own magic?' Hamlet asked.

Thordric thought for a moment. 'No. I've used magic before when wearing it and it wasn't any weaker than usual. I think it was whatever magic's growing the trees that did it.'

Nothing had ever weakened his magic to that extent before. Perhaps he should speak with Vey and Lizzie, they might have heard of a power like that.

16

THE SPRINGS

'Slow down, boy,' Lizzie's voice cracked firmly through the communication device.

She and Vey had gathered together so that Thordric could explain the situation to them both at the same time, but all they had heard so far was that he was in a terrible panic about something to do with trees.

Thordric took a deep breath, looking at Morweena and Hamlet, who were still sitting around the table with him. It had taken them a long time to recover from their surprise at the communicator, particularly when Lizzie had first spoken and Morweena thought she had come back to visit again.

'There's some kind of magic out in the Valley Flats that's making a forest grow. It's spreading so fast that it will probably overrun the town in a matter of days,' he said. 'The worst part is that it seems to be turning people into trees too.'

He told them about the archaeologists who went missing and the human-shaped trees and, while he'd been there, how Tome had vanished to be replaced by a tree.

'And you have no idea what kind of magic is causing it?' Vey asked.

Despite Vey not being able to see him, Thordric shook his head. 'It's not magic like ours. I wasn't even sure it *was* magic at first, but since Hamlet couldn't feel it, I guess it has to be.'

'Your friend Hamlet has no powers?' Lizzie asked.

Thordric looked at Hamlet, who had decided to take great interest in his teacup. 'I haven't felt anything coming from him at all,' he said, feeling as though he were putting Hamlet down somehow.

There was silence for a moment, but then Vey spoke up. 'If you and he were both in the centre of that forest, why didn't you turn into trees?'

'I think we know the answer to that, though we've only just figured it out. We both have a crystal called *Crystos Mentos*. Morweena says it grows naturally in the springs here, though our ones didn't come from there. I think it diverts the other magic away from us, but if you stay in one place for too long trees grow up around you. I was nearly trapped by some.'

'I see,' Vey said. 'Mother, what do you think?'

'I think Valley Edge and the Wanderers are in an awful lot of trouble. I have to wonder, Eric, why it is you're still sitting here dawdling. Find yourself a ship and go there.' They heard Vey wince and listened as his hasty footsteps disappeared from the room. 'And boy,' Lizzie continued to Thordric, 'if those crystals do what you think they do, you should give one to everyone in the area. At least then their lives will be safe. Morweena, you worked at the springs. See if you can get hold of them for him.'

'But Lizzie, I haven't been there for years, and it wasn't exactly under good circumstances that I left, what with the manager's wife chasing me out and—'

'Morweena, this is an emergency. Forget your past indiscretions and pull yourself together.'

Even Hamlet and Thordric drew back from the communicator at the snap in Lizzie's voice. Thordric had forgotten how strict she could be, but given the circumstance, he was very glad of it.

'Boy, make sure that everyone in Valley Edge receives a crystal and then give some to the Wanderers. I'm afraid that until Eric gets there you and Hamlet have to try and figure this out on your own. Do whatever you can.'

The communicator went dead and for a moment the three of them sat there in silence.

'I think we may be in need of a cart,' Thordric said eventually, standing up. 'Morweena, how far away is the first spring?'

Morweena looked up, her eyes bloodshot. 'I think perhaps half a mile, no more,' she said slowly. 'Do you think this will really work, Thordric?'

'I don't know, but we've got to try something.'

Thordric harnessed the horse back to the carriage and fed it a handful of oats. It nudged against him fondly and he rubbed its nose. Morweena came out of the house, dressed surprisingly sensibly in a plain jacket and skirt with only a pair of earrings for jewellery. Hamlet followed her out, now clean and wearing fresh clothes that Morweena had found tucked away in a trunk under her bed. She couldn't even remember who they might have belonged too, but seeing as they'd fit, he hadn't pursued it.

'I've got to make a stop first,' Thordric said as they got in the carriage, wearing a set of fresh robes himself. Once again, he took up the driver's seat and, when everyone was settled, he nudged the horse on.

They reached Lily's house in half the time it would have

taken them on foot. He knocked on the door and waited, but before anyone could answer it, Lily came skipping out from the back garden.

'Thordric,' she said happily. 'Have you come to help me sell apples again?'

'Actually,' he replied awkwardly. 'I wanted to ask your parent's permission to borrow their cart.'

Her face dropped. 'It's not *their* cart, it's *my* cart. I'm the one who has to push it all the way to the docks and back and sell apples from it. And no, you can't have it. Besides,' she added. 'Father is away on *The Jardine* and mother is working at the springs.'

Then she caught sight of the carriage behind him and stared. 'Who are they?' she said, pointing at Morweena and Hamlet, visible through the small windows on the carriage doors.

'They're friends,' he said.

'But I thought I was your friend,' she pouted.

Thordric couldn't help but grin. 'You are. People can have many friends,' he said. Then he turned serious. 'Please, Lily, let us borrow your cart. The people here are in danger and we need it to bring back something to protect everyone.'

She frowned at him, still glancing over his shoulder at the carriage. 'Alright,' she said at last. 'But only if I can go with you.'

'Go with me?' Thordric said, surprised. It hadn't even occurred to him that she might say this. 'It could be dangerous though.'

Lily snorted. 'But you're a wizard. If anything bad happens, you can use your magic to make it better, can't you?'

Thordric wished he could. 'Fine,' he gave in. 'You can come with us if you let us borrow your cart.'

She danced around happily and ran out to open the shed.

He helped her bring out the cart, but then found they had a problem. They didn't have another horse to pull it.

'But you usually push it along with magic,' Lily said. 'Why can't you do that now?'

'That's only around town. I have to take it out to the springs. It's much further and I have to try and drive the carriage as well.'

She stared at him. 'Why don't you attach it to the carriage then?'

'It would be too much weight for the horse to pull. The poor animal's barely keeping up as it is,' he replied, looking over at it. The horse looked back with a pleading look in its eyes.

'Make it all lighter,' Lily said simply.

It was his turn to stare. Why hadn't that occurred to him? Making objects lighter wasn't particularly difficult, all he had to do was lessen the gravity on it. He could halve the weight of everything; that should be light enough.

He attached the cart to the back of the carriage first, summoning some rope to tie it with, adding magic to the knot to hold it in place even more. After that, he felt the weight of everything, including Morweena, Hamlet and Lily, by levitating it all off the ground slightly. The strain made his head ache, but he was able to get the measurement he needed and a moment later he had successfully altered the gravity of it all.

He stood next to the horse, which had been watching him suspiciously, and made it walk on. After a few steps, the horse stopped, surprised by the sudden lightness, and looked around at him. Thordric grinned at it and got back up in the driver's seat.

Now all he had to do was get them to the nearest spring.

· · ·

They arrived as twilight was setting in, but far from being empty as Thordric had thought, the spring was full.

As it was underground, they left the carriage next to an area set aside for use by the guests. With the cart added, the carriage took up quite a lot of room, but Thordric had little time to worry about it.

Morweena led them towards what looked like a stone hut, but once inside they found that it was the start of the steps leading down into the cave where the spring was.

As the small staircase opened out fully into the cave, both Thordric's and Hamlet's cheeks flushed pink. The spring, set a little way back from the stairs, was much larger than either of them had suspected and, to their embarrassment, was full of nude bathers.

'Don't you bathe naked?' Lily asked Thordric, as though he were crazy.

'Of course I do,' he said, swallowing. 'But I don't do it in public!'

'Why not? Everyone looks the same without any clothes on, so why does it matter?' she asked.

'It's simply not decent,' Hamlet cut in, his cheeks turning pinker still. Thordric mumbled his agreement.

Morweena laughed at them. 'They don't bathe like this where they come from, child,' she said to Lily. 'Seeing men and women bathe together naked is very strange for them, I'm sure.'

Lily looked confused, but Morweena shook her head. 'I'll explain it when you're older, child. Now, I must speak with the attendant.'

She started to wander off into a small side cave, but seeing the expressions on the boys' faces, took hold of their sleeves and dragged them with her.

They found a woman standing at a desk with a shelf full of

purple and pink towels behind her, writing in what appeared to be a notebook. Putting down her quill, she looked at them all.

'Morweena,' the woman said, clothed in a calm blue dress. 'I didn't expect to see you here again after what happened with the manager's wife all those years ago. If I remember rightly, she chased you out with a basket of dirty towels.'

Morweena smiled. 'It was rather a bad experience. However, I had to come back due to a somewhat urgent matter.'

Thordric rolled his eyes. Her tone of voice was so casual that she might have been asking the time of day.

At this point Lily came bounding into the room and up to the woman. 'Mother, we need some of the crystals growing at the bottom of the spring.'

'Lily? What in Neathin are you doing here?' the woman said.

'She came with us, Eliza,' Morweena said.

Lily scowled at her. 'I came with *Thordric*,' she said. 'You just happened to be there too.'

'Indeed, child,' Morweena replied. 'Now, Eliza, about those crystals. We really do need them I'm afraid.'

Eliza opened her mouth to respond, then caught sight of the emblem on Thordric's robes. 'You're a member of the Wizard Council,' she said, almost accusingly. 'What are you up to?'

This time Hamlet explained. After half an hour, despite still being suspicious of them and mostly due to Lily's insistence, Eliza closed the spring to everyone but them.

'I hope you don't expect me to dive down and get them myself, though,' she said, escorting the last few stragglers to the stairs.

'Of course not,' Morweena said. 'We'll do that ourselves. Now, strip off everyone.'

122

Thordric and Hamlet looked at her wildly. 'What?' Thordric exclaimed.

'We have to be nude to go into the spring, it's the policy here,' she replied, so seriously that they had no choice but to believe her.

'But there's no one about to make sure that we do,' Hamlet pointed out.

'And what am I?' Eliza said behind him. 'One of those trees you're so panicked about?'

Hamlet gulped.

'If you don't undress then I cannot allow you to enter the spring, no matter how urgent the situation,' she continued.

'Don't worry so much,' Morweena said. 'We'll all be far too busy collecting those crystals to even notice each other.'

17

DIVING FOR CRYSTALS

The spring was far deeper than Thordric had imagined, but given his nakedness, that was a good thing.

He had been the one to strip off first and go in, sprinting so that the others wouldn't have time to see him.

The water was hot, but not scalding, and was so clear that he could see the soft green of the crystals at the bottom from where he swam treading water. Taking a deep breath, he dived down, deeper and deeper until he managed to touch one. Instead of being loose, they were growing in a large and very sharp clump. The part he'd touched was particularly lethal and cut his palm, sending inky redness through the water.

The pain was so sudden that he let go of his breath and had to rise back up to the surface, in time to see a flash of naked limbs and frizzy hair dive past him. A moment later, Morweena's head popped up beside him.

'Be careful, the crystals are sharp,' he said, indicating his hand and summoning a vial of potion from his bag. It was an extremely sticky substance that dried in moments, even in water. Thordric spread it over the cut, and it stopped bleeding instantly.

'How handy,' Morweena said, eyeing up the potion.

'Something I developed myself, but it still needs more work before Vey can approve it,' he replied, trying not to think about how he had made it by accident.

He sent it back to his bag, wondering how to separate the crystals from each other.

'Oh, yes,' Morweena said, watching him. 'You jumped in so quickly that Hamlet didn't have time to tell you. He found these in the storeroom here and said to use them to break the crystals apart before bringing them up. Rocks like this always grow in clumps, apparently.'

She held up a small hammer and chisel. Thordric took it, wondering where Hamlet was now, but two splashes told him that he and Lily had just jumped in.

Trying to avert his eyes from Morweena, Thordric dived back down and began to chisel at the crystals. It was hard work and very slow, for they all ran out of breath quicker from the effort, so it took them several breaths to break off even a small bit of crystal.

After thirty minutes and only a small pile of crystals to show for it, Thordric lost his temper and announced to everyone that he would break them up by magic.

'Absolutely not,' Hamlet said, the heat of the water putting some colour into his skin at last. 'We have to be delicate with these. Besides, they might divert your magic somewhere else and end up damaging the entire spring.'

'But this is taking too long,' Thordric grumbled. 'We need to get these crystals to the people as soon as we can before the forest reaches them.'

'Make some more hammers and chisels, then,' Lily said, as though this had been the obvious solution all along.

Thordric realised it was. If he duplicated his own ones, then he could get them to copy his actions. It would be like having another group of people helping them out.

Another hour later, they all sat around the spring in large purple and pink towels with their fingers and toes thoroughly pruned. Next to them was a pile of crystals as tall as Thordric was.

Morweena had come up with the brilliant idea of putting them all onto several large towels so that, once they were dressed, Thordric could levitate the towels and lift the crystals up the steps that way, rather than risk using magic on the crystals themselves.

It worked well and soon they had filled the cart full of them, with more having to be put in the carriage, leaving very little legroom once everyone was inside.

As they had been putting the crystals in, Thordric had summoned some super oats for the horse so that it would be feeling strong enough to get them back quickly. He also adjusted the weight of the cart again, as the crystals weighed much more than he'd thought. The horse nudged him happily and, as soon as everyone was inside, he stepped up to the driver's seat and took the reins again.

Though it was fully dark by now, Thordric saw an outline of trees from the corner of his eye. The forest was very close. He didn't think they could wait until morning; they had to distribute the crystals the moment they got back.

Reining the carriage in at Morweena's house and asking Lily to take care of the horse, Thordric went around the corner to see Mr Henders.

He knocked on the door and Mr Henders opened it, dressed in his nightclothes.

'I'm sorry to disturb you, Mr Henders, but I need your help. Your brother's too if he's in,' Thordric said, stepping inside.

As if in answer to his question, Grale appeared down the stairs. 'What's all this about?' he complained. 'Can't you see it's the dead of night?'

Thordric pulled a sceptical expression. According to the clock on Mr Henders' wall, it was only a quarter past nine.

'Sit down for a moment, both of you,' he said, walking into the lounge and taking a seat himself. They sat, Grale none too happy about it, and Thordric explained the crisis that everyone was in.

'That's all very well,' Grale said afterwards. 'But what do you want us to do?'

'You're going to help me wake everyone up and bring them to the docks,' Thordric said, trying hard not to sound imperious.

'Of course I'd be happy to assist, sir, but how are we to do this?' Mr Henders asked.

Thordric's cast his hands wide. 'Well...' he began dramatically.

Bright red flames appeared in front of every house in Valley Edge, illuminating the night and letting out such pops and crackles that even the deepest sleeper jumped awake.

Thordric admitted he was impressed. Mr Henders and Grale, for all their lack of experience and training, were doing a marvellous job.

After teaching them the basics of how to do it, he gave them each a section of Valley Edge to work on, taking the area by the docks himself so that he could make sure it was the only apparent safe area. It wasn't long before the people came running in great groups, flooding every inch of space on the docks.

Dressed in his only set of ceremonial robes and with Morweena, Hamlet and Lily all standing by him next to the huge pile of crystals that he had once again levitated into place, he waited until the crowd had come to a natural silence; every eye focused on him.

If it hadn't been so important, he felt he would have blushed.

'Residents of Valley Edge,' he began, increasing the volume of his voice so that it carried to the very back. 'I am Wizard Thordric, representative of the Wizard Council. I am here to tell you that you are in danger. There is a forest, controlled by a form of magic of which we know little, spreading at an alarming pace. Soon it will reach here and most of your homes could be lost, but that is not all. If you get too close to it, then you are likely to be transformed into trees yourselves. The only means that will protect you from being consumed by it are these crystals beside me. Every person in Valley Edge must carry one on their person at all times and, those of you who have animals, I suggest you make sure you take enough for them, too.'

There was silence for a moment, but then someone in the crowd jeered at him. 'You expect us to believe that?' the man said. '*Nothing* grows in Neathin Valley, there's no chance that a forest could spring up out of nowhere.'

There was a murmur of agreement from the crowd and some even started to walk away, but Thordric held up his hands.

'If you don't believe me then feel free to go out into the Valley Flats and see for yourself. But I urge you, please take one of these crystals with you, else you might not return.'

The man in the crowd sniffed but took a crystal anyway

and left the docks. Seeing this, everyone else came forwards to take one, demolishing the pile within minutes. It was working.

Now all they had to do was go back to the Wanderers' hide out. He hoped it wasn't too late for them.

There was no chance of sleep that night so, before he set out again, Thordric drank some of the alertness-inducing tea that Hamlet had given him in the forest. He made it an extra strong brew to try and counter the effect that the *Crystos Mentos* had on it, but when he arrived at the hide out, he was so awake that he thought his eyes might pop out his head.

Thankfully, the forest was still some way off from the hide out entrance, though he couldn't be sure if it had reached the caves closest to it yet.

Reaching out to touch the rock, the illusion vanished to reveal the hole underneath. He went in, landing on the platform leading to the staircase.

Once he got to the main cave, he found most of the Wanderers there waiting.

'It's you,' one of them said. 'We were expecting Tome. Where is he?'

Thordric winced. He wasn't looking forward to telling them that their leader had mysteriously turned into a tree while helping him. 'Before I explain, please take these stones. Everyone must have at least one. Keep them on you at all times,' he said.

The wizards all eyed him suspiciously but did as he said.

The youngest of the group, a wizard named Roomer, spoke first. 'Has Tome been up to something again?' he asked. 'He hasn't been arrested, has he?'

'Don't be ridiculous,' another one broke in. 'Tome wouldn't

do anything risky while the boy's here, ready to report back to the High Wizard at a moment's notice.'

Thordric almost wished that Tome had been arrested. At least it would be easier.

'Nothing like that has happened,' he began. 'Unfortunately, it's much worse.'

'Worse?' Roomer asked. 'How so?'

Thordric tried, as best he could, to explain to them all what had happened with Tome and Yim in the forest.

'He's a tree? Yim too?' the one who had interrupted before said. 'Well, I knew he was getting a bit stiff in his old joints, but to actually turn into wood...'

Thordric blinked. What did that remind him of? Stiffness in the joints...like arthritis, he supposed. Wait, what was it Lizzie had said to him?

It wasn't arthritis she had; her body seemed to stiffen up inexplicably every ten days, since she'd been to visit Morweena. Had she somehow been in contact with part of the forest? But that couldn't be right, that'd been weeks and weeks ago, and she hadn't said anything about going to a dig site.

'Are you quite yourself, boy?' Roomer asked, noticing that Thordric's face had gone white.

'I'm fine,' he said, the effects of his tea wearing off. 'I just need to rest for a moment.'

His body was heavy and, moments later, he collapsed on the ground.

When he awoke, he found that the Wanderers had put him to bed, in the same cave that they had given him before. Hearing movement, he sat up and saw the door open. Roomer came in carrying a tray of tea and biscuits.

'How long have I been asleep?' Thordric asked, suddenly in a panic.

'Relax, boy,' Roomer said. 'It can only be half an hour at most.'

Thordric breathed deeply, his pulse returning to normal. 'My bag,' he said, pointing to where it lay on the floor. 'The long-distance communicator is in it.'

Roomer put the tray down and rooted around, finally pulling out the communicator. Thordric noticed that a petal on the blue flower poking out the top was slightly bent, but it straightened out again at the touch of his hand.

He pressed the button on the communicator's side and spoke into it. 'Lizzie? Are you there?'

18

CARVED PYRAMIDS

'Spell's rebounded, boy!' Lizzie said through the communicator. 'I was deep asleep! Still, I suppose it must be important.'

'It is, though it's probably not about what you think,' Thordric replied, sitting up in the bed with Roomer watching him curiously.

'Go on, boy,' Lizzie said. 'What is it?'

Thordric thought for a moment, wondering what to say. 'When you were here, did you go anywhere out of Valley Edge?'

'No. Not even to the springs, though given this reoccurring stiffness I wish I had of done. The only places I visited were in Valley Edge.'

Thordric scratched his chin, noticing that his beard had filled out a bit more. 'Did Morweena give you anything from the Valley Flats at all?'

'Not that I recall, but one of her friends did give her a gift. Said he'd got it from a local merchant and thought she'd like it.

Some kind of carved pyramid. He gave me one as well, actually,' she said.

Thordric narrowed his eyes. 'This friend of hers wasn't called Tome, was he?' he asked.

'Now that I think about it, I believe it was, yes. Didn't you say one of the Wanderers was called that?' she asked.

'Yes, he's the one who was with me in the forest.'

'I see. I remember now that she seemed to think very highly of him, but something about him made me uneasy, as if he had magic but didn't at the same time. Of course, if he was a Wanderer then it all makes sense.'

'That's not all he is,' Thordric replied. 'You were right to feel uneasy about him; he's one of the biggest crooks I've ever met. I bet he didn't say where the merchant got those carvings, did he?'

'No, why? What are you thinking, boy?' she asked.

'Tome has a reputation of stealing things and then selling them on. If those archaeologists brought back something from the site and he took it...'

'That's all very well, but what makes you think it's the carvings that he gave to Morweena and I?'

'Your arthritis, or whatever it is. Before Tome turned into a tree, he said that his body was starting to feel stiff. If that carving of yours is from the dig site, then it might be what's causing it.'

'If that's the case, boy, then why hasn't Morweena complained of such, then?'

Thordric thought for a moment. As far as he knew, Morweena hadn't had any *Crystos Mentos* in the house before they had given it out to everyone. Then why *hadn't* she been affected?

Wait. She'd had the dust from the springs. It must've had

the same qualities as the crystals themselves. If that was true, then it *was* the carving that'd been causing Lizzie's arthritis.

'Lizzie, would you mind giving me that carving?'

'Not if it's important. It will take a few days, though. Eric's already left and there's not another ship for a while.'

'I'll summon it, then,' he said. If it was from the dig site, then it might be the key to stopping the growth of the forest.

'Boy, that's ridiculous. It's too far; not only will you strain yourself, but you don't know what the thing looks like.'

That was true and summoning only worked when the caster knew what the object looked like. 'Does it look the same as the one that Morweena has?' he asked.

'Yes, but hers is black and mine is white. Other than that, they're identical.'

'Then all I have to do is imagine her one white. It will work, I promise.'

Roomer went with him back to Morweena's to make sure that he got back safely. He was still feeling weak and had to sit inside the carriage while Roomer drove.

The forest was closer now, barely metres away from the hide out and so, to protect the horse, they had tied several crystals to the harness. The horse had been rather glad to see Thordric appear, because the sudden closeness of the trees had been making it nervous again. After he had given it some more super oats and water, it ran straight into a canter.

The carriage, with Thordric inside, bounced along behind it even more than usual, but they made good time and arrived back at Morweena's within the hour.

'Thordric, dear boy, you're safe,' she said, floating up to him with at least a dozen crystals around her neck. 'And who is this fine gentleman?'

Roomer blushed and opened his mouth to speak, but Thordric cut in.

'He's a friend of Tome's,' he said, quickly. 'He wants to help us find a way to stop the trees from spreading.'

'But I thought that's what these crystals were for?' she said, as Hamlet came down the stairs.

'They'll only stop us turning into trees, Morweena,' Hamlet said, squeezing past her to stand next to Thordric. 'We have to find a way to get to the source and stop it there. Right, Thordric?'

'Yes. I don't know how to do it yet,' Thordric started, 'but I believe Morweena's got something that can help us.'

'I have?' Morweena said, looking rather blankly at him.

'That's right. Lizzie's got one too.'

'I still don't...' she said, making Thordric sigh.

'Tome gave the two of you presents, didn't he?' he said. 'A carving of some kind?'

Morweena pulled at her hair. 'Oh, yes...' she said. 'I remember now. Lovely little thing it was, too.'

'Well?' Hamlet said.

'Well what, young man?' she asked blankly.

Thordric swallowed, trying to keep his temper. 'Where *is* it?'

'Where?' she replied. 'It must be somewhere in the house, but I'm not sure exactly where. It *was* quite a few weeks ago, you know.'

At this point, Thordric was certain that Morweena was the most infuriating person he had ever met. 'Fine, we'll just have to search the house.'

Without even bothering to consult Morweena, he told Hamlet and Roomer what Lizzie had said about the carved pyramids. 'This one should be black,' he said, while Morweena found it best to go and make tea. 'It's about four inches high, and the point is quite sharp.'

They each took a separate room to search. Thordric took

the lounge, Roomer took Morweena's bedroom and Hamlet took the bathroom. As Thordric had only managed to clear his bedroom, the rest of the house was still piled high with Morweena's many possessions. Searching for such a small object would be difficult, but he knew that Hamlet would probably have it worse because he didn't have any magic to speed up the process.

In the lounge, Thordric thought it best to shrink everything as he checked it so that he could be certain the pyramid wasn't behind anything. Inches of dust covered every surface, and by the end of it, he had plenty more crystals of *Crystos Mentos*, enough to make him wonder if it wouldn't have been easier to craft them here instead of getting them from the springs. Still, that wasn't important now. As long as everyone was safe, that was all that mattered.

Once he'd finished, the room looked completely different. With everything having been shrunk and neatly stacked into one corner, he went to check on Hamlet.

He found him hanging over the bath, coughing and sneezing so much that he hadn't even heard Thordric come in. There was a mist of dust in the air, which Thordric immediately collected into a ball and pressed into another crystal.

However, there was also a strong smell of perfume, so strong in fact that it made him feel quite faint. 'Hamlet,' he gasped, forcing the window open to its fullest. 'Are you alright?'

Hamlet turned to him and sneezed, oodles of red smoke shooting out of his nostrils. 'I...I,' he began, but sneezed again. 'I took some potion she had lying around; it said it was for allergies, so I thought it would help me with the dust in here.'

'A potion? Do you still have the bottle?' Thordric asked suspiciously.

Hamlet held out a small red bottle, with 'Anti-Allergy' written on a plain label stuck to it. Thordric recognised the handwriting as Tome's, another gift bestowed by him to Morweena.

He half felt that Tome deserved to be a tree by then.

Opening the bottle, he sniffed it. He couldn't smell a single one of the herbs used in a real anti-allergy potion. Looking at Hamlet, still sneezing, he summoned another potion from his bag.

'Here,' he said, giving it to Hamlet. 'This should take away the effects of whatever that was and stop the dust from affecting you so badly too.'

Hamlet smiled weakly and unscrewed the cap on the vial. In one swig it was gone and with it, all signs of the smoke coming from his nostrils. 'Thanks,' he said.

Thordric clapped him sympathetically on the shoulder. 'So, did you find anything in here so far?' he asked.

'There's a few more potions, but no pyramid yet,' Hamlet replied. He showed Thordric the rest of the potions and watched as he took great delight in pouring the whole lot down the sink. Several strange scents filled the room, but at least they didn't have any effect on anything.

'If I ever manage to turn Tome back again, I'm taking him straight to the station house to be charged with theft and selling fake goods,' Thordric said savagely. 'Now, let me have a look here too.'

He turned to the stack of jars, clay figures and books lining the entire wall, forcing the dust off it all and shrinking each one down to barely a third of its original size. Hamlet watched, amazement spreading across his face.

'You make it look so easy,' he said, a little sadly. 'I often wish that I could use magic, but I suppose you've got to be born with it.'

Thordric turned to him. 'Well, to use this kind of magic, yes. But not everything uses the power of the wizard. Look at these crystals, for instance. They've got their own magic. It works the same way with potions, too. Anyone can make an effective potion if they know how, wizard or not.'

'Really?' Hamlet asked.

'Really,' Thordric said. 'When I was first being taught magic by Lizzie, she showed me how to make them and, since she's got no powers herself, it must be true. She also said that if you're around magic for a long time, you're sometimes able to feel whether someone is a wizard or not. That's how she knew I was one.'

'Then...would you be able to show me some things? About how to make potions, I mean?'

'If that's what you want. Once I'm back at the council you can come and see me anytime you like. Vey as well; he likes teaching others, so I'm sure he would help you. Don't be fooled into being his test subject when he's working on something new, though...'

Hamlet laughed as Thordric shook his head, remembering all the times Vey had used him to test out his potions.

After another few minutes, he had shrunk everything in the room apart from the bath, toilet, and sink. So, the pyramid wasn't in there, either.

They wandered out and bumped into Roomer, who was also yet to find anything. That left only two places, since Morweena had been adamant that the pyramid wasn't in her bedroom. The kitchen and the loft. Neither Thordric nor Hamlet wanted to be around her just then, so it was down to Roomer to check the kitchen where she they had told her to stay. They, on the other hand, had to go up to the loft.

'I'm sure I saw the trapdoor here somewhere,' Thordric said, looking up at the ceiling on the top floor. It was a high ceiling and rather dark, with shadows looming about everywhere.

He summoned up a handful of small blue flames and spread them across the ceiling. The shadows crept backwards and there, to the left, Thordric spotted the handle to the trap door.

'How are we going to get up there?' Hamlet asked, craning his neck to see it. 'I haven't seen any ladders around at all.'

'We don't need one,' Thordric said, levitating Hamlet up to the ceiling. 'Are you high enough?'

There was a grumbled reply and the trap door opened. A long, silver ladder fell down from inside as Thordric hastily moved Hamlet to the side so it wouldn't hit him.

'How very impractical,' Hamlet said, taking hold of it and climbing the rest of the way up. Thordric followed, sending a few of the fires up through the hole so they could see inside.

He soon wished he hadn't.

H anging down from the loft's roof were cobwebs so thick Thordric had to cut through them to see what was behind, but that wasn't what concerned him most. Morweena certainly hadn't been lying when she'd said the loft was full. In fact, both he and Hamlet now saw that that had been a gross understatement.

Among mountains of jumble, ranging from abandoned sculptures to derelict clocks, there were yet more books. Whoever had stored them there had obviously decided that stacking was beyond their ability, or else had failed to see the importance of trying to preserve what looked like ancient manuscripts.

Thordric picked one up. He gasped. 'Hamlet, look at this!' he said, grabbing Hamlet's sleeve and pulling him through a cobweb.

As the soft, sticky web caught his face, Hamlet shrieked and flapped his hands apart, jumping back so violently that he landed in another one. He shrieked some more and began tearing desperately at his clothes. Startled, Thordric reacted by summoning a bucket of water and splashing it all over him. Hamlet froze, water dripping from his nose, and took several deep breaths. 'Thank you,' he said quietly. 'I don't know what I would have done if you hadn't done that.'

Thordric brought a clean handkerchief from his pocket and offered it to him.

Hamlet took it gratefully, drying his sopping face. 'I'm afraid I've always been terrified of webs like that.' He shook himself. 'So, what was that book you were about to show me?'

Thordric blinked; he'd almost forgotten about the book in his hands. 'Here,' he said, holding it out.

'This is...how did Morweena ever get hold of something like this?'

'I'm not sure, but she'll have a lot of questions to answer when we get back downstairs.'

They scoured the rest of the loft, with Thordric collecting all of the dust and webbing in a great ball, while neatly stacking and shrinking the jumble into one pile. They found some more interesting books to keep out as they went, but no sign of the carved pyramid. He hoped Roomer had had better luck, but given Morweena's love for chatter, he supposed not.

'Well, I guess we should head back downstairs,' Hamlet said at last, gloomily sitting by the trap door and letting his legs dangle down. 'If only I could get a glimpse of this thing, then perhaps we could find out precisely which ancient peoples it belonged to.'

'We will find it, Hamlet. It must be here somewhere; she wouldn't have thrown out anything that Tome gave her. Honestly, I don't think she's *ever* thrown anything out in her life, judging by all of this.' Thordric gave one last sweep with his magic, collecting any remaining dust. The ball of it all, floating in front of him, was now larger than his head. 'Let me make some more crystals. It would be a shame to waste precious material.'

He put pressure on the dust ball as he'd done before but, instead of the pale green of *Crystos Mentos* that he expected, this crystal was clear and colourless. He let it go in surprise and it fell heavily onto his foot, making him utter a stream of colourful language that made Hamlet turn even paler than usual.

So, none of the books or other things up here had any dust from the springs on them. If Morweena hadn't had an interest in them, then who had?

Sliding down through the trapdoor, holding on to the ladder, they climbed back down to the second floor. They could hear Morweena talking away in the kitchen, with a few polite grunts coming from Roomer.

Levitating the books they had found behind him, Thordric headed downstairs with Hamlet following.

'Ah, there you are,' she said to them as they walked into the room. 'Any luck?'

They both scowled at her, so much that she drew back slightly.

'Oh dear,' she said quietly. 'Perhaps you should both have some tea.'

'Morweena, please. We don't have time for tea,' Thordric replied, throwing the books on the table with a loud bang. To his surprise the table wobbled slightly and fell to one side as something shot out from under it.

They all stared. It was a smooth, black pyramid with some kind of writing carved into the sides. Thordric picked it up, noticing that as he did so the *Crystos Mentos* around his neck glowed even brighter than it had done in the forest. This was it.

'I remember, now,' Morweena said, clapping her hands together with delight. 'The table leg was broken some weeks ago, but when Tome fixed it for me it was a few inches shorter. That pyramid turned out to be just the right size to fill the gap.'

'You mean it was in here all the time?' Thordric said, grinding his teeth.

'Yes,' she replied, making him put his hand to his temple. At least now he could use it to summon the one Lizzie had and free her from that strange illness.

He gave the pyramid to Hamlet, who sat studying it seriously. Thordric took out the long-distance communicator and placed it on the table, its flower thankfully still healthy.

'Lizzie,' he said into it, pressing the button on the side.

'There you are, boy,' came her reply. 'Did you find it?'

'Yes,' he said. 'I'm going to try summoning your one now. Where is it?'

'It's on the side in the kitchen, by the stove. Be careful, boy.'

Thordric smiled. 'I will.'

He looked at the black pyramid, imagining it made of white stone instead, and pictured it where Lizzie had said her one was. It wasn't easy, for despite the amount of *Crystos Mentos* in the room, the strange magic of the pyramid kept on pushing his concentration back. Trying harder, he had a moment, briefly, where he saw the one in Lizzie's kitchen clearly. It hadn't been much, but it was enough.

A moment later, the white one appeared on the table, right next to the black one. They all stared at it. Thordric breathed a little easier.

He turned back to the communicator. 'It worked,' he said. 'I'm going to send over some of the crystals we're using to divert the magic. They should clear any remaining effects this thing had on you.'

Taking out a handful of *Crystos Mentos* that he had in his pocket, he placed them on the table and willed them back to the place by the stove where Lizzie's pyramid had been.

'Did it work?' he asked her.

'Yes, boy, I've got them. Good lu—'

Her voice was overridden by the alarmingly close sound of creaking wood.

Thordric and the others rushed to the windows. Trees had sprouted up all around them, right through the heart of most of the houses and more were growing every moment. The forest had reached Valley Edge.

'We've got to leave,' Thordric said, grabbing the books on the table and shrinking them down so that they would fit in his bag. 'Hamlet, you keep hold of the pyramids, don't let them out of your sight!'

He rushed out the door, the others following closely behind. The people outside were in a panic, running everywhere trying to get away from the trees, but there was nowhere to go.

A loud whiny from behind the house told them that the trees had started to grow around there too, terrifying the horse. Without thinking, Thordric ran around to the makeshift stable he had built and let the animal out, trying his best to soothe it. It calmed eventually, enough for him to lead it around to where the others were still standing.

'What do we do now?' Roomer asked, looking in every direction for a way out of the expanding forest.

'The only thing we can,' Thordric replied. 'We've got to go into it. Back to the dig site.'

'But what will happen—' Morweena broke off as a large dark shadow passed overhead.

Thordric looked up. Above them all, floating proudly in the sky, was the entire fleet of the Ships of Kal, with *The Jardine* at their head. As they moved in at full sail, hovering a good few metres shy of the tallest tree, they saw that Vey was aboard *The*

Jardine, just visible at the stern. He climbed up onto the side, balancing himself with his magic.

'People of Neathin Valley,' Vey's voice boomed, causing the ground to shudder. Everyone stopped, awed at the sight of twenty floating ships hanging above them. 'You must evacuate Valley Edge now. The wizards of the council will assist you with boarding these ships. All animals and livestock will be evacuated too,' he continued.

Thordric was sure he had glanced in his direction as he stood protectively by the horse.

'Please make your way to the nearest ships. There is no need for alarm as there is room for all.'

As he finished his speech, they saw that there were groups of wizards from the council aboard every ship and, by the few startled screams, they had started levitating people up onto the decks. Thordric grinned as Vey beckoned in their direction.

Still holding the horse tightly, Thordric levitated Morweena up to *The Jardine*, then did the same for Hamlet and Roomer. Afterwards, with Vey's help, he and the horse were levitated up too. Despite the horse panicking slightly, they both landed safely on the deck.

'I'm glad to see that you're all alright,' Vey said, clapping Thordric on the back. 'And you, Aunt Morweena,' he continued as she tried to embrace him. He nodded to everyone in turn. 'Truly, I am glad you're all safe. I was worried I wouldn't make it in time.'

'But how did you get here so quickly?' Thordric asked, walking the horse to one of the stables that had been erected on deck.

'I worked out a way to improve upon the potion that keeps the ships afloat. They can sail much faster now,' Vey replied proudly. Then his expression dropped. 'You look tired. Why don't you get some rest? We'll handle the rescue, so don't worry.'

'But we've got to go back to where the dig site was,' Thordric said, desperately. 'It won't stop if we can't find a way to disable the magic.'

'The people are safe for now, Thordric. There are no towns or villages near here for several hundred miles. A few hours' sleep isn't going to hurt you. Any of you,' he said, turning to the rest of them. 'Now, let us do our job.'

Before Thordric or anyone else could object, he pushed them towards the door leading down to the cabins with a strong gust of wind. The door opened as they reached it but Thordric, getting there first, fell down the steps and landed face down on the carpet.

'Whoops,' he heard Vey say from outside.

Thordric gritted his teeth angrily as Hamlet helped him up, while Roomer and Morweena strolled casually down the steps. 'Which cabins shall we take?' she asked, looking around at the large hall. She caught sight of one of the portraits of Kalljard hanging on the wall. 'Oh, dear. I don't like the look of him at all,' she declared. 'Who is he?'

Hamlet snorted as Thordric tried very hard not to cry out in disbelief. 'Shall we find our old room?' Hamlet asked cheerfully, taking Thordric's sleeve and dragging him as far away from Morweena as possible.

It struck Thordric then how much Hamlet had changed since being in Neathin Valley. Somehow, he seemed far less serious than before. It suited him.

They made their way back to 'The Rookery', though by the time they reached it Thordric realised how long it had been since he'd last had a decent bath and, on top of that, how filthy his robes were. 'Here,' he said, taking the books they had found out of his bag and giving them to Hamlet, resizing them as he did so. 'See if you can find out anything about those pyramids.'

'Of course,' Hamlet replied.

With that, Thordric left the room. Despite his tiredness, his feet found their way to the baths. He went in and pulled off his robes, jumping straight into the warm water.

He was about to fetch the soap when there was a shriek beside him. Turning, he saw a young woman, hastily covering herself with a towel. He blinked and looked at the sign on the door. It read 'Women's baths.'

He gave up and sank below the water.

20

SHIP SHAPE

Now clean and having slept for several hours, Thordric rose to see if Hamlet had made any headway in figuring out what the two pyramids were for.

The young archaeologist was across the room, his nose buried deep in what looked like one of the oldest books they'd brought with them. The title read 'Ancient Cultures of Dinia'. He had never given much thought to who had lived on the continent before them, though he was glad that Hamlet had taken such an interest in the subject. Without him, they would all be lost for what to do.

'Hamlet?' he said. There was no response, so he said it a bit louder.

'Oh, you're awake,' Hamlet said, jumping so badly that he almost dropped the book.

'Have you learnt anything yet?' Thordric asked him, indicating the two pyramids standing next to the pile of books by Hamlet's bed.

Hamlet worked a crick from his neck. 'I'm not sure. The markings on the pyramids seem to match up with some of the characters from a tribe called the Ta'Ren. I have heard of them before, and it's true that they lived around here...but they weren't believed to have any form of magic at all. As far as I know, they didn't even use potions.'

'But whatever's causing this must be magic,' Thordric protested.

'I know,' Hamlet said. 'I'll keep reading; perhaps they developed something later on in their history.'

'Alright, but don't tire yourself out, otherwise Vey will probably force us to take sleeping potions and lock us in here until we've recovered,' Thordric said. 'I'm going up on deck to see how things are going.'

He left the room, turning into the corridor and following it up and around to where it joined the main corridor. He was glad to see more people hurrying around, though he hoped he didn't meet the young woman he'd accidentally shared a bath with. Even the thought of it made a pink tinge rise to his cheeks.

Up on deck, he saw that the stables were now full, with as many horses and cattle as could comfortably be housed in them. Vey was standing by them, rubbing the nose of Thordric's horse.

'This is a good horse you've got here,' he said as Thordric approached. 'Though you should be careful that he doesn't eat too much.'

'He?' Thordric asked, wondering why he hadn't thought to check himself.

'Yes, and his name's Koleson.'

Thordric's eyes widened. 'You can talk with him?' he asked.

Vey laughed. 'No, though I wouldn't pass up the opportunity to try and learn how.'

Thordric raised an eyebrow and Vey laughed some more. 'I helped his previous owner on board, said he had been stolen a few days ago. Fortunately for you, the owner just found himself with an awfully large debt to pay off and wouldn't have been able to keep him anyway. The chap asked if we could continue taking care of him.'

'It wasn't me who stole him,' Thordric said defensively, going up to pat Koleson's neck. 'It was Tome. He also stole the carriage he was harnessed to.'

'I guessed as much. When we finally manage to turn Tome back, I think I'll be having a rather long chat with him,' Vey said, scratching his short beard.

'You really think you'll be able to?' Thordric asked.

'I don't see why not. He might have been transformed into a tree, but at least it's another living thing. If he'd have been turned to stone, I would be doubtful, but the simple fact that he's still technically alive gives us a chance,' he replied.

He stopped, being signalled to by another wizard from the council. He went over to the ship's side and looked over, frowning. 'Thordric,' he shouted over to him. 'It looks like we may need your help here after all. We've still got a lot of people to get on board and the trees are getting taller.'

Thordric went over and looked himself. The tops of the trees were brushing up against the hull, but if the ships sailed any higher it would be hard to see the people down below. They had to get them up now, before the trees broke through the ships.

'We'll do a group levitation and get them all up in one go, I think,' Vey said, counting the number of people. 'We need to form a physical chain to synchronise our magic, so everyone join hands.'

All the wizards onboard, including Roomer, who had apparently been helping out while Thordric was asleep, joined hands making a chain of twenty-two strong. Focusing their magic on the crowd waiting desperately below the trees, they willed them all to be levitated upwards as a single group.

Thordric had never known the council to synchronise their magic in such a large group before; even with three people it was likely to be unsteady. If one person lost their concentration, then the whole chain would collapse and, if that happened, the magic could backfire with some dangerous results.

However, everyone was trying their hardest and so they managed to get the people on deck without incident, except for when Thordric's sleeve got caught in another wizard's neck chain as they parted hands. The chain was pulled down and the wizard's head hit the side of the ship with a rather loud bang. It was only then that Thordric realised what happened and tried to untangle himself but slipped over and nearly pulled his arm out of its socket.

'Well, you seem to be on good form today,' Vey said, separating them and summoning an ice pack for the wizard's head. The wizard took it and hurried as far away from Thordric as he could get. Vey chuckled.

'You're not doing so bad yourself,' Thordric replied. 'That was really risky, making a chain that big. If anything had gone wrong...'

'But it didn't. Yes, it was risky, but I knew it would be fine if we were all working together to save people. With determination like that, our powers were almost linked anyway. The chain gave everyone that nudge to complete it.'

'I don't think Lizzie would have approved of that explanation,' Thordric said.

Vey's face went pale at the mention of his mother. 'We don't need to tell her about it,' he said hastily. 'It would only make her worry, anyway.'

He got up and stood on the edge of the ship again, looking across at the rest of the fleet. Thordric followed his gaze and saw the wizards on the other ships all waving their hands at him in a signal.

Stepping back down, he sighed, breathing deeply. 'It looks like we've got everyone. Let's head higher and see how much the forest has spread everywhere else.'

He called up to the sailors to adjust the sails before heading into the captain's navigational cabin, which also contained the helm. Thordric followed.

'Let's take her up then, Captain,' Vey said, talking to a man who looked curiously like Lily.

'Aye, sir,' the captain said, turning the great wheel in his hands. Thordric felt the ship move, catching the updraft of the wind. The front wall of the cabin was painted the same as the ones in the viewing room, so it gave the effect of looking through a window. Soon Thordric saw that they had risen right above the clouds.

Still staring at the captain, he felt a question slip off his tongue. 'Are you Lily's father?'

'Aye, I have a girl called Lily. You know her?'

'I've helped her with the cart a few times,' Thordric said.

The man smiled. 'She loves that apple cart of hers, won't let anyone else touch it.' Then his face turned serious. 'Is she safe? My wife, too?'

'Yes, they're both safe. They should be on one of the ships, though I can't say which. Everyone in Valley Edge had crystals to protect them from turning into trees, we made sure of it.'

The man let out his breath. 'Thank you. I'm Captain Mavers, by the way, but you can call me Jal. My cousin's a wizard like you, you know. Haven't heard from him in some time, not since that big to-do with Kalljard a few years ago. His name's Rarn, have you met him?'

Thordric smiled weakly. Wizard Rarn used to be Kalljard's assistant, though all that meant was that he'd acted as housekeeper. When Thordric and the inspector had questioned most of the council after Kalljard's death, Rarn had been quite uncooperative, to the point where he had kept some valuable information secret.

The last time Thordric had seen Rarn was the day Vey had revealed to the council that both he and Thordric were half-wizards. Thordric remembered animating the stone figures in the hall and setting one after Rarn. He could still hear the screams as it had chased him out of the hall and down the corridor.

'He's doing well,' Vey said, rescuing Thordric. 'He's currently working at our Wizard Council Training Facility with our young wizards.'

'Good to hear it,' Jal said, turning his attention back to steering the ship.

Thordric tried very hard not to snort. Vey had set Rarn to work at the Wizard Council Training Facility all right, but it was to attend to the cleanliness of the baths and toilets rather than teaching.

Vey went with Thordric back to 'The Rookery', leaving the other wizards to see that everyone on board had found a place to sleep.

Hamlet was still reading when they went in, only looking up when he heard Vey.

Vey smiled at him and held out his hand. Hamlet took it shakily. 'You're the High Wizard, aren't you?' he asked.

'An unfortunate title, I admit,' Vey said, pulling a face. 'Please call me Vey. I hear you're the young archaeologist who was sent to the dig site where this all started.'

'Yes, sir...Vey,' Hamlet replied. 'But as I told Thordric, the trees had already started growing when I arrived. All I know is that whatever is in the main excavation area is likely the cause of all this. That's where I saw that everyone else had been turned into trees. They were all gathered in the centre.'

'I'd heard as much,' Vey said grimly. He looked at the pyramids by the bed and picked one up, but no sooner had he touched it than his hand started to change colour to a dark, woody brown.

Quickly, Thordric grabbed it and threw it on the floor, pressing a handful of *Crystos Mentos* into Vey's hand. The crystals glowed brightly, and his hand turned back to normal.

Vey swallowed and looked at them both. 'I see what you mean. Perhaps I should keep one of these crystals myself,' he said, looking nervously at the pyramids. 'Though it seems that the effect is much faster on wizards than normal people, else my mother would likely be a tree by now.'

He turned to Thordric. 'I'm glad you figured out that this was causing her illness. If she'd have kept it any longer...'

Suddenly, Hamlet threw down his book in anger.

'I don't understand. None of the cultures I've read about so far even had a trace of magic,' he said, half-shouting. 'I don't even know how it was triggered, aside from these things being something to do with it.'

He kicked at the pyramids and then shrieked as pain shot through his toes. 'I'm not even sure what they're made of. It looks like stone, but I've never seen anything like it, especially the white one.'

'You should take a break, Hamlet,' Vey said. 'I believe it's coming up to supper time, so perhaps we should all make our way down to the dining room.'

'I suppose you're right,' Hamlet agreed grudgingly.

Tucking the pyramids under his bed, he followed Vey and Thordric out of the cabin, locking the door behind him.

With so many people on board, the queue for the dining

room extended halfway down the corridor. Everyone waiting spoke in short, hurried whispers, but they fell silent when they saw Vey approaching. Vey simply smiled and got in line with everyone else, ignoring Thordric's hints and grumbling stomach to use his title to skip ahead of them all.

As they were waiting, Thordric felt a sharp poke on his spine and turned to see Lily standing there with her mother.

'You didn't tell me your father was captain of *The Jardine*,' he accused.

She pouted. 'Being captain doesn't make him any more important than the other sailors,' she said. Her mother flared her nostrils but kept silent in front of Vey.

Thordric inhaled sharply. He had just remembered what she'd told him about her brother going to the dig site weeks ago. Why was nobody mentioning him?

21

HAMLET'S HISTORY LESSON

'Eliza,' Thordric said to Lily's mother, 'have you had any word from your son?'

Eliza stared at him. 'I don't wish to talk about him,' she said coldly.

'But Lily told me he had gone with some archaeologists to the dig site,' he pressed. 'Surely you've heard what happened there. Aren't you worried?'

'If that boy has managed to get himself turned into a tree, then it is his own fault. I told him not to go, but he refused to listen.'

'He's a half-wizard, isn't he?' Thordric asked. 'And why did you just call him "that boy"? Surely he has a name?'

'He's called Kal,' Lily said, glaring at her mother. 'But only Father calls him that.'

'He was an orphan,' Eliza said, sniffing as though she had caught a whiff of something nasty. 'My husband found him wandering around in Jard Town, claiming that he was Kall-jard's son.'

Everyone gaped at her.

Vey and Thordric met each other's gaze. Sure, there were rumours that Kalljard had fathered children, but no one had taken them seriously for even a moment. Kalljard was adamant that wizards should never have families because the male children would always be half-wizards.

'Of course, I never believed him,' she continued, 'but Jal did. Said it wasn't safe for him there; if Kalljard knew he had a son, and a half-wizard at that, then the boy would be in real danger.'

'You adopted him?' Thordric said.

'We did, but I'm sure you can see why I was so reluctant to do so. To be the mother of someone like that...' she paused and took a breath. 'He was always trying to use his magic, but of course it never worked. When Lily here was born, I was afraid what he might do to her. I didn't want him in the house, so when he came of age last year, Jal tried to apprentice him onboard these ships. But the boy is disobedient, and when he heard there had been a discovery out in the Valley Flats that was believed to be highly magical, he ran off in search of it. I suppose he thought it might strengthen his powers or what not. Either way, he's gone now.'

Thordric's face had grown hot. This woman's cold indifference to her son's safety simply because he had been a known half-wizard made him angrier than he'd been in a very long time.

Vey, however, was standing next to him quite calmly. 'I see, madam. Once we resolve this current issue, we shall take your son into our care. You need not concern yourself with him any longer.'

The queue for the dining room had moved considerably by then, so they parted from Eliza and Lily. Lily had wanted to sit with them, but Eliza decided it was best to take their food back to the cabin rather than sit in the dining room and take up precious space.

After they had piled up their plates with food and found a place to sit, Thordric banged his plate on the table, making everyone, including Hamlet, jump. Vey smiled at everyone pleasantly and they all looked away again. He turned to Thordric.

'I know how you feel, Thordric,' he said, an unusual tinge of sadness in his voice. 'But being rash and scaring the whole ship will only make everybody panic more.'

'But she...even if he...how could she be like that?' he managed at last.

'Plenty of people are still like that,' Vey said. 'Isn't that why you came here? To educate people so that they know there is no difference between the abilities of wizards regardless of how they were born?'

'Yes,' Thordric said, pushing his fork around his plate. 'And I failed.'

Vey laughed quietly, making Thordric and Hamlet stare. 'Had it not been for the current situation below us, I might have agreed with you. However, I should point out that you've barely been here a week and, in that time, have found three half-wizards, two of which now know that they can come to the council for training should they wish to. Not to mention that the Wanderers, apart from Tome and Yim, have all agreed to come back to the council to see the changes for themselves.'

'They have?' Thordric said, blinking. Then he remembered how close the trees had been to their hide out last time he was there. 'Wait, we need to go and get them on board too; the forest was—'

'Relax, Thordric,' Vey said. 'They're already onboard, on this ship too, I believe. We picked them up before we got to Valley Edge. Many of them helped us with the rescue, but unfortunately they'd all retired to their cabins by the time you came out.'

'So, everyone should be safe for a while?' Hamlet said, pushing his empty plate away.

'Yes, for at least a few days, but there should be enough provisions on board to last us a week,' Vey replied.

They were all silent for a moment. The dining room emptied around them and soon they found themselves alone. At last, Thordric spoke.

'Do you really think that Kal could be Kalljard's son?'

Vey tugged at his beard again. 'Perhaps, but I do find it hard to believe. Still, I have someone in mind who might know, though it would be best not to summon him until we've cleared up this mess.'

'Who?' Thordric asked, now calm enough to eat.

'Oh, just a past friend of yours,' Vey said, with a nonchalant flourish of his hand. 'And, incidentally, the boy's uncle, since Eliza and Jal adopted him.'

Thordric stared. 'Rarn? He would know such a thing as that?'

'As someone who made it his business to haunt Kalljard everywhere, I'm sure a rather indelicate detail like that would hardly have slipped past him.'

They finished their meal and left the dining room, making their way back to 'The Rookery'. The corridors were silent now and they had seen no one on their way there. Vey left them once they had reached the cabin, telling them specifically to get some rest and not stay up all night trying to figure things out.

They had both told him adamantly that they had no intention of working any more that evening and, satisfied, he'd strolled off. As soon as he'd gone, however, Hamlet took out the pyramids again and opened his books.

Feeling rather useless, Thordric took out the books he had brought with him for the trip; the potion book and plant identification book that had both been written by Lizzie's husband.

He opened the book on plants, wondering if there was anything in it about rapid growing trees that he might have missed, but somehow, he ended up staring at the very last page. It depicted one of the Watchem Watchems; small creatures that lived in forests and disguised themselves as bushes and sometimes trees. He had seen them before, during his training with Lizzie when she'd taken him to her country house near Watchem Woods, named after them.

Staring at the sketch showing the long, branch like limbs and pointed fingers, he realised something. He had seen a picture of them recently, though not as detailed. It had been simplified into just the basic shape, but he knew it had definitely been one.

He got up and picked up one of the pyramids, making Hamlet jump and fall off the bed. Examining the symbols carved into each side, Thordric gasped. There it was, the symbol for the Watchem Watchems.

Now the question was, what would a Watchem Watchem have been doing in Neathin Valley thousands of years ago, if not more?

'Hamlet,' he said, as Hamlet tried to pick himself up, accidentally treading on a book and ending up sliding forwards into a split. 'Have a look at this.'

He pulled his friend up and showed him the picture in the book and the symbol on the pyramid.

Hamlet stared, confused at first, but then he cried out and hit his head with his fist. 'How could I have been so idiotic?' he said, choosing some curse words that even Thordric had never heard before.

'What is it?' Thordric asked.

Hamlet sat down and flicked through the book on ancient cultures, finding the page he wanted and holding it out for Thordric to read. There was a picture of a Watchem Watchem, though it was slightly different to the ones Thordric had seen before. It appeared taller and its hands were larger.

'When I looked before,' Hamlet explained, 'I only thought to look for human tribes in the area. It didn't occur to me that another species would be involved.'

'But how would the Watchem Watchems have survived in Neathin Valley? They live in forests and depend on them entirely,' Thordric protested.

'Neathin Valley hasn't always been so barren. When all the tribes lived here, around six thousand years ago, there were plenty of forests. The Ta'Ren used to gather most of their food from them. It's believed that they had a close bond with the Watchem Watchems.'

'Then how did the Valley Flats become how they are now?' Thordric asked.

'There was another tribe living there at the time, called the Neathers. They wanted more land and, during a war with the Ta'Ren, burnt all the forests down. Without the trees to hold the water, the land dried up. Eventually they took over and became the ancestors of most of the people living in Neathin Valley today.'

'That still doesn't explain this magic, though,' Thordric said.

'Actually,' Hamlet said slowly, a spark in his eyes, 'I believe it might. I still need to check, but I think the Ta'Ren and the Watchem Watchems created it together, to restore the forests,'

Hamlet said. 'But if they were all killed before they could activate it, then that would be why the Valley Flats stayed barren.'

'Then...that's why this magic feels so different to ours!' Thordric exclaimed. 'It's because it wasn't made by humans at all.'

Hamlet smiled, rather wearily. 'It still doesn't tell us what these pyramids are for, though,' he said.

'No,' Thordric agreed. 'But I think I know how to break through those roots covering the main excavation site now.'

He dashed out of the room before Hamlet could say anything and hurried along the corridors, looking for Vey's cabin, but soon it occurred to him that he had no idea where it was.

Hoping to find one of the other Council wizards, he made his way up on deck. Apart from a few sailors on their night watch, it was empty, but he saw light coming from the captain's cabin and so decided to ask him if he knew where Vey was.

He knocked politely on the door. Jal opened it and, when he saw Thordric, a grin spread across his face. 'You're looking for the High Wizard, no doubt?' he said.

'Yes, actually...'

Jal opened the door wider, beckoning him in. In the corner of the cabin, tucked up in a tight ball on the floor, was Vey. He was snoring loudly. 'Your reverence,' Jal said, prodding Vey gently on the shoulder. Vey groaned sleepily. 'Your reverence, young Thordric is here to see you.'

Slowly, Vey sat up, his eyes bleary. 'You should be in bed, Thordric,' he said, letting out a long yawn.

'You won't say that after what I've got to tell you,' Thordric replied excitedly.

'Go on, then,' he said, standing up and stretching with yet another yawn.

Thordric told him about what he and Hamlet had discovered, so rapidly that Vey had to stop him several times to go back over certain things.

'So, these Ta'Ren were working with the Watchem Watchems?' he asked, once Thordric had managed to finish.

'Yes,' Thordric said.

'And you have a plan to break those roots covering the excavation site where you think this magic is coming from?' Vey asked, intrigued.

'I think so,' Thordric replied. 'I need to find the Watchem Watchems and ask them to come with me.'

'The ones from Watchem Woods?'

'Yes, they know me, after all,' Thordric replied.

'In that case, we need to find some way of getting you there and back quickly.' It was Vey's turn to grin. 'Come with me. I think you'll find what's in the cargo hold *most* interesting.'

22

DINIA'S JEWEL

Vey led Thordric into a corridor that he had never been down before; the wooden walls were painted red instead of the standard purple decorating the rest of the ship.

At the end was a large set of double doors, filling the entire wall. It was inlaid with precious gems and, carved in the middle where the doors joined together, was a detailed impression of Kalljard's face, shaped down to the individual hairs on his beard.

'Impressive, isn't it?' Vey said, stopping in front of it. 'Though I don't care for the subject much. Still, I've got plenty of time to have it changed.'

He put his hand on Kalljard's nose and pushed against the wood. The doors opened slowly to reveal a large black space within. With Thordric following, Vey went inside and closed the doors again behind them. Then he summoned four great white fires and put them in each corner, revealing a large room with unpainted beams.

'This is the cargo hold?' Thordric asked.

'Indeed. I was surprised when I found it, for I thought it was empty at first,' Vey replied.

Thordric blinked. The room certainly looked empty to him.

Vey caught his expression and smiled. 'Look closer,' he said mysteriously.

Thordric did so, even walking over to each corner and checking the ceiling to make sure there wasn't anything small or painted that he'd missed. 'I still don't...' he began, but then turned and walked to the middle. The metallic smell of strong magic hung in the air.

He put his hand out and it hit something hard.

'Well?' Vey said, watching him.

'It's an illusion to make the object look like part of the room. There's not even a shadow or anything. It's perfect.'

'Thank you, it took me quite a few hours to get it right,' Vey said airily. 'I lifted the original to see what was underneath, you see, but I wanted to know what you made of it, so I replaced it. I suspect that the original was cast by Kalljard; it was much stronger than that one.'

'What's it hiding?' Thordric asked eagerly.

'Why don't you find out?'

Thordric did so, feeling for the edges of the illusion and tugging at them gently. Nothing happened, but then he hadn't really expected it to, knowing Vey. He tugged again, much harder this time, and the shape of something large began to show through. With one last tug, the illusion broke completely.

He stood back and gaped. In front of him was a pleasure boat, small in comparison to the giant Ships of Kal, but filling most of the room, nonetheless. Thordric wondered how he hadn't walked into it when he'd been inspecting the room.

It looked as though it had been crafted from the same fine woods as the ship and had carvings all around the side. At the prow, acting as a figurehead, was a life-sized wooden statue of Kalljard.

'Thought a lot of himself, didn't he?' Vey said, rolling his eyes at the statue's severe stare. 'Anyway, she's also a floating vessel and I tinkered with her elevation fluid the same as I did with the fleet. Since she's smaller, she might be able to go faster. We could get to Watchem Woods and back in a day.'

'We?' Thordric asked, surprised.

'Of course. I believe I'm right in saying that out of the two of us, I'm the only one who can sail.' Thordric scowled at him briefly, making Vey chuckle. 'Then it's settled. You, Hamlet, and I shall disembark first thing tomorrow. Now, *please* go to bed and rest. I know how grumpy you get in the mornings.'

'You're no better yourself, particularly if you plan to sleep on the floor of the captain's cabin again.'

'Precisely,' Vey said. 'There's no sense in both of us being in a foul mood, is there?'

The three of them rose early the next morning and met down in the cargo hold.

Hamlet swooned when he saw the boat, rubbing his hand along her hull and then climbing aboard to do the same to the mast and rigging. 'She's beautiful. What's her name?' he asked, looking for it on the side.

Thordric choked. He'd had no idea that Hamlet liked boats so much, considering how seasick he had been when they'd first met onboard *The Jardine.*

'Strangely, she doesn't have one,' said Vey, levitating their belongings onto her deck.

'I heard it's awfully bad luck to sail a boat that has no name,' Hamlet said darkly.

'I heard that, too,' Vey said, climbing aboard himself and helping Thordric up after him. 'Why don't you name her?'

'Me?' Hamlet asked. 'But I have no idea what to call her.'

Thordric shrugged at him. 'Make something up,' he said, unhelpfully.

Vey shot him a merciless look. 'Call her whatever feels right,' he said to Hamlet.

Hamlet stood on her prow, looking at every detail of her. 'How about...*Dinia's Jewel?*' he said at last.

Thordric and Vey looked at him. It was perfect, as though it had been her name all along somehow. 'Shall we paint it on then, Thordric?' Vey asked.

They got back off and looked at her side, discussing how big to write it and in what style. In the end, they each took a side and painted it on in slanted, bold writing in solid black.

'We shouldn't have any problems with her now,' Vey said, standing back to admire her. Then he turned to Hamlet and Thordric. 'Shall we set sail then?'

With all three of them aboard *Dinia's Jewel* once more, Vey and Thordric used their magic to release the panel in *The Jardine's* bow, ready for them to sail out. Taking the ship's wheel and activating her elevation system, Vey led her out of the cargo hold and into the bright clouds below, immediately soaking them all.

They reclosed the panel and set off, going below the clouds to make out the direction they needed to go. As they sailed above the treetops, they saw that Valley Edge had been completely overrun. It barely looked like a town anymore.

Not long after they'd started moving, Hamlet's travel sickness made its appearance and he had to retire to the cabin with his books, as all the potion that Thordric had given him had been left at the dig site with the rest of his belongings. Only Vey and Thordric were able to stay on deck, though at the speed *Dinia's Jewel* was moving, they both found it difficult to stay standing.

In the end, Vey summoned chairs from the dining hall of *The Jardine* and magically stuck them to the deck so that they didn't have to keep picking themselves up off the floor.

The mountains and rivers that Thordric remembered floating gently over on his way to Neathin Valley had become no more than a blur. He didn't think he had ever seen anything move so quickly as *Dinia's Jewel*.

By the time the afternoon arrived, he found that they were already nearing Jard Town and, as Watchem Woods was only a day's carriage ride away, they would reach it in a matter of minutes.

They passed straight over the Wizard Council's crescent-moon-shaped building and the station house without slowing, though Thordric had been tempted to ask Vey to stop at Lizzie's to tell her what was going on. Still, there wasn't time for that and soon Jard Town passed under them with *Dinia's Jewel* not even slowing for a moment.

They reached Watchem Woods barely ten minutes later. Vey thought it best to anchor the boat next to his mother's house, near the very mouth of the trees. As soon as the boat stopped moving, Hamlet appeared again, still slightly shaky on his feet. He saw the house beside them and stared.

Thordric wasn't surprised, for he had done the same thing the first time he'd seen it.

The house was so long that it extended into the woods themselves, though Thordric knew it only went a short way in, and it was several stories high. Inside, though you couldn't tell from looking at it, there were so many corridors and rooms that it was easy to get lost. Thordric had done that, too.

'Shall we go?' Vey asked, smiling slightly as he looked at the house. 'It's been an awfully long time since I've been here,' he remarked. 'Perhaps I'll take a short break here after this is all resolved.'

He sighed wistfully and led them away into the woods.

It was nice being among trees that didn't try to trap them, Thordric thought, and he couldn't remember the woods ever being as vibrant and full of flowers and bushes as they were now.

Every plant was a different colour, ranging from bright red stalks with small, black flowers to long grasses coloured a fine silver. He saw that one of the plants he'd often collected here, a spindly dark green one that grew large purple bulbs instead of flowers and was named *Big Man's Nose*, had spread everywhere. There were also a great many bushes of blues, purples and yellows growing in each direction.

Finding the Watchem Watchems, whose favourite game was to disguise themselves as foliage, might not be as easy as he'd thought, particularly when he remembered that aside from Vey's father, he was the only one who had ever seen them up close before.

They walked further and further in; Thordric trying to remember the exact spot where he had seen them last and hoping that they hadn't forgotten him. If they had, then he could forget asking them for help.

Suddenly there was rustling all around them. They stopped and stood still.

'How did you get them to come to you before?' Vey asked, while Hamlet shook slightly next to him.

'I didn't. They just appeared,' he replied.

'They're not...aggressive, are they?' Hamlet asked quietly.

Thordric laughed and a strange gurgling sound answered him. Everyone looked around. 'They're here somewhere,' he said, searching the bushes for any sign that they might be something other than they appeared. 'And no, they're not aggressive. They do have sharp fingers, though.'

A bush wobbled in front of him. He went over to it, making it look as though he was about to pick one of the leaves. The bush shuffled away from him, quivering even more. The gurgling sound came again, and he found himself surrounded by more bushes.

Vey and Hamlet leapt back from him, eyeing the bushes with a mix of fear and curiosity. Thordric looked over at them, and then down at the gurgling bushes.

'It's alright,' he said, kneeling down. 'They're friends too.'

The bushes all became quiet for a moment, but then moved off to surround Hamlet and Vey instead.

'Thordric, what are they doing?' Hamlet said, rather desperately clinging to a nearby tree.

'They're checking to see if you're safe. They won't reveal themselves otherwise,' Thordric replied.

The bushes gurgled affirmatively and moved back from Vey to stand behind Thordric. They seemed to be making some angry hissing sounds, too. Thordric pulled a puzzled expression.

'They don't trust you,' he said to Vey. Meanwhile, the bushes around Hamlet gurgled excitedly.

'But I haven't done anything,' Vey protested. 'I haven't been in these woods for nearly twenty years, and even then, I...'

His eyes widened slightly, and he mouthed an 'oh'.

'What is it?' Thordric asked with a sinking feeling.

'I did practice some magic in here a few times, only for a few hours or so...I think some of it ricocheted and hit one of them. And I may have uprooted a tree.'

The angry hissing grew louder. Thordric put a hand to his brow.

'That must be what's upset them so much,' he said. 'Do you remember where this tree was?'

'I believe so,' Vey replied, creasing his brow. 'It was slightly further in, east a way.'

'Then we should try and right it,' Thordric said. He turned to Hamlet, who seemed to have passed out on the floor. The bushes had decided to climb onto him, almost covering him completely. 'I'll carry him if you lead the way,' he said.

'What about the Watchem Watchems?' Vey asked.

'They'll probably follow us to make sure that you really do right the tree; though I'm not sure what to do if it's dead.'

'Can't you convince them that it's important for them to help us?' Vey pleaded as the bushes hissed at him again.

Thordric looked at them and shook his head. 'That will only make them worse,' he said.

He went over to Hamlet, gently pushing the bushes off and then levitated him into the air. 'Where to, then?' he asked.

Vey slumped his shoulders and directed them straight on.

23

WATCHEM WATCHEMS
EVERYWHERE

The uprooted tree was still there and, to everyone's delight, alive.

It hadn't been displaced completely, only enough to make it fall over, and so the roots had kept growing, despite how much they'd been exposed.

It was a large tree, almost as tall as the house, but the trunk was rather thin. Small clumps of mushrooms covered the bark, as well as several different lichens. It seemed to Thordric almost a shame to move it again, but if that's what made the Watchem Watchems happy, then that's what Vey had to do.

Standing back to assess it, Vey deepened the hole around the roots slightly so there would be room for all the new growth. The bushes gurgled as they watched him, but it wasn't an angry sound. Encouraged, he levitated the tree and turned it back to its proper upright position before planting it in the ground. He filled in the remainder of the hole around the trunk and, for good measure, took a vial of rejuvenating potion from his pocket and sprinkled it on the soil around it.

'Well,' he said, turning to Thordric. 'Has that made them happier?'

In answer, the bushes all quivered, slowly losing their leaves, and shrinking into small, skeletal forms that looked like they were made up of branches. Each one was the same colour as the bush it had been disguised as, and they had short beards of leaves.

'I don't believe it,' Hamlet said, conscious again. One of the Watchem Watchems poked him in the shin with its spindly finger. He yelped and it gurgled, running around him in circles.

'They're really something,' Vey said, as two of them decided to climb up his robes and sit on his shoulders, pulling his long hair and poking suspiciously at his beard. 'How do we explain what we need them to do?'

The question earned him a jab in the ear form the one sitting on his right.

'All we have to do is tell them. From what I've gathered, they seem to understand our language well,' Thordric replied.

Vey and Hamlet looked at him.

'Perhaps you should explain it, then. It looks like they trust you the most,' Hamlet said, edging away as the one who had poked him stopped running around and danced up by his legs again.

Thordric pulled out his plant book again and knelt on the floor. He opened it on the page detailing the Watchem Watchems and held it out so that they could see it. They all stopped what they were doing and ran to look at it.

The gurgling they let out at seeing the picture was so deafening that several birds took flight. A few moments later, another bush, moving slower than the others had, came towards him as the Watchem Watchems parted to let it through. It transformed gradually and Thordric noticed that the leaves around its faced formed a long, trailing beard. Two small tears of sap rolled down its woody cheeks.

Thordric looked at it and then at the picture in his book. Now he understood. This was the Watchem Watchem that Vey's father had sketched all those years ago. It must have been very close to him to stand still for so long while he took down the detail.

'Hamlet,' he said softly, as though speaking any louder in front of this one would be disrespectful. 'Do you have that book of ancient cultures with you?'

Hamlet nodded and pulled a book out of his bag, passing it to him.

Thordric took it and turned to the page on the ancient Watchem Watchems, holding it alongside the other book so that they could see the similarity between themselves and the ancient ones.

They all crowded around him once more, leaving a slight gap around the elderly one as a mark of respect. 'A long time ago, we believe that your ancestors had their forest destroyed by a human tribe. They decided to work together with a different human tribe to restore the forest, sharing their magic to create a device which would make the trees grow once more,' he explained, turning the page to the Ta'Ren, and letting Hamlet tell them how they'd used the forest alongside the Watchem Watchems.

'The device was never used, for both the Watchem Watchems and the Ta'Ren were killed by the other tribe,' Thordric continued, listening to their dark hissing at his words. 'But recently it was activated by accident and now the forest that's growing has taken over the whole region, endangering the lives of many species by trapping them or turning them into trees. I believe that since your ancestors helped make it, you can help us stop it.'

The Watchem Watchems stared at him for a long time after he'd finished. He decided to sit back and let them discuss it in their strange gurgling way, but they made no sound for a long time.

Then, after what seemed an age, the elderly one stepped forwards. It picked up the book on ancient cultures and looked at the pages itself, flicking between the ancient Watchem Watchems and the Ta'Ren. Suddenly, it threw the book down and crossed its arms together before flinging them apart, letting out a long hiss.

'What's the matter with it?' Vey asked, glancing from Thordric to the Watchem Watchems.

'It doesn't want to help us, not when it was a human tribe that caused all this in the first place,' Thordric replied.

'What do we do now then?' Vey said, but a loud hissing interrupted him.

The other Watchem Watchems were communicating with the elderly one, making strange gestures with their arms. One of them even picked up the book on plants and held it up to it, poking the picture that Vey's father had drawn and then pointing at Thordric and gurgling.

The elderly one endured this for a few minutes more, while Hamlet, Vey and Thordric watched the strange interaction, both apprehensive and curious. More tears of sap rolled down his face to harden in his beard of leaves and, finally beaten, it threw its hands down and stood in front of Thordric. The others did the same.

'What just happened?' Hamlet asked, still keeping his distance from them.

'I'm not certain,' Thordric began. 'But I think they reminded him what Vey's father was like and that helping us would be like helping him.'

'So, they've all decided to come with us?' Vey said.

In response, the Watchem Watchems swarmed at them.

On board *Dinia's Jewel,* the Watchem Watchems flooded into the cabin, refusing to stay on deck for even a moment.

Hamlet, to his terror, found that his travel sickness had once again returned and so had to join them in there.

All Vey and Thordric heard was a whimpering sound followed by their loud gurgling. Thordric had forgotten how mischievous they could be and began to feel rather sorry for him.

Still, only a few hours later they were back in Neathin Valley, heading straight for the dig site.

They closed in, with Vey trying to manoeuvre the boat around the trees, some of which had now reached the clouds. Floating above the middle of the main excavation area, they lowered the anchor.

Thordric decided to shimmy down it, waiting for Vey to levitate the Watchem Watchems to him. Just as he had finished summoning fires to light the way, he heard them running out of the cabin. They were still gurgling, and as he watched, they jumped off *Dinia's Jewel* and found themselves floating down towards him in the air. A few of them even did somersaults or tried to run, but as they noticed the giant trees around them, they all fell still.

Next, Vey lowered Hamlet down and, feeling rather guilty, Thordric noticed a few scratches and bruises on his friend's hands and face. Finally, Vey shimmied down the rope himself and all of them, with their *Crystos Mentos* glowing brightly to counteract the forest's magic, made their way through the trees and thorn bushes towards the main excavation site where the wooden bodies of the archaeologists could still be seen.

As Thordric showed Vey the middle where all the roots had grown, the Watchem Watchems hissed again. Thordric felt his body go cold. If even they were reacting like that, then something had gone very wrong.

'This is the spot where you couldn't cut through?' Vey asked, bending down to touch the roots. Before he could lay a finger on them, however, the elderly one leapt forwards and knocked his hand away. A great thorn grew up right where it had been.

'I don't seem to be having much luck with touching things from here,' he said, glancing back and forth from his hand to the thorn. He turned to the elderly one and bowed to it slightly in thanks.

'It didn't do that before when I touched it,' Hamlet said. He walked forwards and reached his hand out. The Watchem Watchems watched him quietly but didn't try to stop him. Nor had they needed to, for nothing happened.

'It must only do that to people with magic, then,' Thordric said. He turned to the Watchem Watchems, kneeling down to speak with them again. 'Can you help separate the roots for us?'

They huddled together, gurgling among themselves and then they all spread out around the roots, forming a ring. The elderly one stood in the middle, balancing on top of the roots.

To Thordric's surprise, thorns shot up around it, narrowly missing its legs, but it didn't seem to notice.

The thorns travelled down the roots until all of them were surrounded, but none of them moved so much as an inch. Instead, they raised their arms and moved them from side to side, a shower of leaves sprouting forth and showering down on the roots. More and more leaves came down, until the Watchem Watchems were almost buried by them.

Then the leaves started pulsing with a dark green light that radiated out across the whole excavation site. As quickly as it had started, it stopped, vanishing with the leaves.

The Watchem Watchems all fell down, lying so still that Thordric wasn't sure if they were even alive. Only when the one closest to him reached up and tugged at his robes did he realise that they were simply resting.

He breathed deeply but noticed that both Vey and Hamlet were frowning. He followed their gaze and saw that the roots were still there, looking exactly as they had done a moment earlier. Had the Watchem Watchems' magic failed?

'It didn't work,' Hamlet breathed next to him, dropping to his knees and then hurriedly scurrying away as a sapling sprang up between his legs.

'Wait,' Vey said, stepping forwards to put his hand on the roots again. Nothing happened. 'They've disabled the magic on them.'

'Then we can break through?' Hamlet asked, but Thordric had already summoned all his magic and sliced through them before he could finish speaking.

The roots fell apart as Thordric caught the elderly Watchem Watchem in his arms to prevent it from getting caught under them. Underneath was a large, circular stone slab, connected on the outside to the veins of gold running through the ground. It looked as though it was made of a similar stone to the carved pyramids, though it was a different colour to both of them.

Deep lines had been etched into its surface, tracing two triangular patterns that spiralled in upon themselves. In the middle of the patterns were two holes, also triangular in shape, but narrowing down to a point at the end.

Hamlet traced them with his fingers and then reached for his bag, rummaging around in it until he found the two pyramids. They seemed to be exactly the same size and shape as the holes, to be inserted point down.

He looked at Thordric and Vey, who both gave him an encouraging nod. Taking a deep breath, he put one in each hole, hearing them click into place. A deep grinding came from below them and the stone slab split apart to reveal a tunnel leading underground.

DOWN INTO THE DEPTHS

The tunnel sloped down so steeply that it was all Thordric could do not to let his feet slide. It seemed to have been dug in a spiral, so that the end would likely be directly under the main excavation site.

Thick roots grew around the sides, but as he and the others had already found, touching them made them grow large thorns just as the ones above ground had done.

Even the Watchem Watchems were having trouble; they had resorted to forming a chain between Thordric and Vey, holding on to their robes for stability. Only Hamlet was managing not to slide, for he'd put on a pair of boots that had spikes built into the sole, making his feet grip deep into the soil. He'd retrieved them from his tent on the surface, but as he only had a single pair, Thordric and Vey had to go without.

Thordric was considering how to make them when his foot caught a large rock and he stumbled forwards onto his face. As he fell, the chain of Watchem Watchems, who were holding onto his and Vey's robes, were flung forwards too. Vey, feeling his balance go, reached out, and latched onto Hamlet, whose boots were no match for the weight of them all, and soon they found themselves shooting down the tunnel on their stomachs.

The end of the tunnel came into view far too soon for Thordric to prepare himself. With a hard crash, they all landed in a heap on the floor, made of polished stone. The chamber they were in resonated, though Thordric found his ears were ringing for a different reason.

As they all sat up, he felt a large cut down the side of his face, though it didn't seem to be deep. Rummaging around for the sticky potion in his bag, he pulled it out and poured it along the cut. The bleeding stopped almost instantly, but his head still throbbed.

Vey hadn't fared much better; his robes had ridden up over his head, revealing a set of silken undershorts decorated with flowers that, in any other situation, would have made Thordric snigger. His legs were all scratched and bruised and, as he stood up, he wobbled to one side.

The Watchem Watchems had all bounced off Thordric and been propelled further into the room. As they picked themselves up, their joints sounded like someone dropping a large pile of firewood.

Hamlet, who was unscathed but now bare foot, took one of Thordric's light globes out of his bag and shook it. As it illuminated the room, he looked around and gaped.

'Do you know where we are?' he gushed, as Thordric and Vey grumbled to each other about their injuries and exchanged potions to help with them.

'No idea,' Thordric said, still concentrating on his wounds.

'We're in a chamber that no one has been in for thousands of years,' Hamlet replied, excitedly, running his hands alone the smooth stone floor, delicately engraved with the same type of markings as the pyramids.

'Actually,' Vey said, hobbling over to where Hamlet was

standing, 'I think you'll find that someone was here quite recently.'

Hamlet frowned as Vey pointed to the centre of the room, lifting the light globe so that it shone in that direction. There was a tree growing there, not much taller than Hamlet himself.

They all crowded around it, taking in every detail of its split trunk and branches spread out like it was reaching for something. 'It's like the others,' Thordric said, noticing a bulbous bit on one of the branches shooting up from the centre, like a head. 'This tree was a person.'

'One of the archaeologists?' Vey said, examining the branches to see if any tools were trapped in them.

'No, I was told that the team only had five members, excluding me,' Hamlet said. 'Whoever this is, he's not one of them.'

Thordric felt his body go cold. Kal, Lily's brother, had been at the dig site. 'I think,' he began, 'that this could be the boy claiming to be Kalljard's son.'

Vey stared at him; his eyes narrowed. 'But what was he was reaching for?' he asked, gazing around the room, which was empty apart from the tree.

'Perhaps he put an illusion over whatever it was, like Kalljard did to *Dinia's Jewel*,' Thordric said. 'With all this strange magic about, I can't tell.'

'Neither can I,' Vey replied. 'We could combine our magic and try a lifting spell. It should dispel an illusion if there is one.'

Thordric agreed and together they tried sweeping the room with their magic, but neither of them could summon their powers at all. 'I can't even get a hold on anything. It's just like what happened before, when I tried to use magic in the forest,' he said.

The Watchem Watchems gurgled and ran over to him, the elderly one being carried by two of the others. They set it down in front of the tree and, after examining its branches for a few minutes, the elderly one made another gesture with its arms. There was more gurgling from the others as they formed a ring around a space on the floor in front of the tree.

Raising their arms as they had done on the surface, leaves once again began to fall on the floor, again emitting a dark green light. As if in response, the stone floor began to glow a deep blue and, in the space where the leaves had fallen, a large black orb seemed to float out of it like a blob of ink.

It rippled once and then hardened, levitating in front of the outstretched branches of the tree. The Watchem Watchems fell to the floor, their magic disappearing once again.

'What is this?' Thordric asked, helping them all back up to their feet.

Vey looked at the orb, his reflection visible on its surface, horribly distorted. 'This is wizard magic, from our time,' he said, frowning at it. He looked at the tree again, and his eyebrow shot up.

'Thordric, I believe you were right. This tree must be the boy. That's the only explanation I can come up with for magic of our era having been used on this,' he said. 'He must have used his own magic in conjunction with what was already here.'

'But why?' Hamlet asked, as Thordric spoke at the same time.

'Is that even possible?' he said. 'We can't use any of our magic down here.'

Vey tugged at his beard, considering both. 'We know that he announced himself as Kalljard's son. If he wanted to prove himself as a wizard and knew that the magic here was strong, then perhaps he tried to harness it. If he tried it before the magic was activated, then his magic would have worked.'

'You think he was the one who caused all of this?' Thordric asked.

'I can't be certain, but, yes, I think he did,' Vey replied a little sadly. 'Of course, I doubt he knew what it would do.'

Hamlet took in the orb, along with the tree and the Watchem Watchems as they huddled together around Thordric again. 'You know, something has been annoying me for a while now. If the Ta'Ren and the ancient Watchem Watchems wanted to grow the forest back, why did they make it turn people into trees as well? It doesn't strike me as something they would have wanted.'

The Watchem Watchems looked at him and gurgled approvingly.

Vey had the answer to that too. 'I don't think they did. I suspect that when young Kal used his magic on it, something went wrong, and it altered the original spell. It's what comes from being left untrained, I'm afraid.' He folded his arms, thinking. 'If we can find a way to break through his magic, then I believe the Watchem Watchems may be able to take care of the rest.'

A tingling from the stone at Thordric's throat reminded him that the *Crystos Mentos* had the power to divert the ancient magic. They had brought several pouches of it with them to be on the safe side and suddenly, he found himself with an idea.

'I think I know how to do it,' he said. Vey and Hamlet turned to him. 'We can't use magic here because it's being overridden by the other magic. If the *Crystos Mentos* diverts that same magic away from us to stop us from becoming trees, then maybe it can divert the magic surrounding the orb.'

He went over to his bag and pulled out all of the pouches of *Crystos Mentos*. Giving some to Hamlet and Vey, he shook the remaining ones out into his hand and then held the crystals to the orb, forcing them against its surface. 'Press them to the orb like this,' he said to the other two.

They did so and then waited for more instructions. 'I think we should try to smash the orb with magic,' he said to Vey, unsure if it would even work. Concentrating together, they both sent a wave of magic crashing into the orb. There was a sharp cracking sound, and everyone was knocked to the floor by a sudden wave of ancient magic, scattering their crystals everywhere.

Recovering, Thordric saw that the orb was covered in cracks, but he was too exhausted to use his magic on it once more. Spotting a crystal beside him, he picked it up and threw it with all his strength. The black surface of the orb shattered, shooting out lethal shards across the room.

Scooping as many of the Watchem Watchems behind him as he could, he curled up into a ball, shielding them from the shards.

There was silence for a moment.

'Is everyone all right?' he said, sitting up. He saw that Hamlet had thrown himself behind the tree, which was now embedded with shards all over. Thanks to that, he was once again unscathed.

To his relief, he found that Vey was too, aside from a slight scratch on his cheek. He and the other Watchem Watchems had run back towards the tunnel and hidden there until the rain of shards had subsided.

'We're fine,' they both replied, with Vey adding, 'how about you?'

'I don't think any of them got—' Thordric began, but he stopped as he felt something wet and sticky on his side. He felt it with his hand, looking down at it. *Blood.*

'Spell's rebounded!' Vey said, coming back into the room and seeing the red on Thordric's hand and robes. Thordric went dizzy and fell back towards the floor, but Vey quickly knelt and caught him gently around the shoulders. 'Hamlet, fetch me Thordric's bag,' he said urgently.

Hamlet ran to get it and brought it back, kneeling by Thordric's side. 'We need to get to the wound,' he said. 'I need a knife or something sharp to cut through his robes.'

He searched through the bag, but there was nothing he could use. Then a gurgling came from behind him, and he turned to see a Watchem Watchem there, flexing its pointed fingers.

Hamlet moved aside and it stepped forwards, tearing through Thordric's robes with one swipe, revealing the wound. It was very deep and, as he wiped away the blood, he saw that the shard was still inside. He hesitated, looking at Vey.

'If I pull it out, it will bleed even more,' he said, remembering what his professor had once told him about the tribes that had used arrows as their main weapon. Pulling one out of someone who'd been shot only opened the wound more.

'Not if we're quick,' Vey replied, easing Thordric down to the floor and then pulling two vials out of the bag, one of them the sticky potion that Thordric had used on his cut.

'Here,' he said, giving Hamlet the other one. 'Pour that one on the wound first; it will cleanse it. Then pull out the shard. I'll pour this sticky one over it and the wound should close.'

Hamlet gulped at him but then gritted his teeth. He unscrewed the cap on the vial and emptied its contents right over the wound. It fizzled a dark purple, mixing with the blood and turning brown.

Taking a deep breath, he then took hold of the shard and tugged it hard. Thordric screamed and fell back in a near-faint, but the shard came out cleanly.

Vey quickly pushed Hamlet aside and poured the sticky potion right inside the wound, covering it completely. They waited.

25

ALL TOGETHER

Thordric coughed and rolled onto his side, sitting up. He looked at Vey and Hamlet, surrounded by the Watchem Watchems. They were all looking at him.

'What happened?' he said, stretching and feeling a dull ache below his ribs on one side. He looked down and saw that his robes had been torn and, underneath, was a dark purple scar.

'You had a piece of shard stuck in your side. I pulled it out, remember?' Hamlet said, concern on his face.

Thordric found that he *did* have a memory of a sharp pain. That must have been it.

'We cleaned the wound and sealed it,' Vey said. 'That sticky potion of yours is quite handy; I'm not sure what we would have done without it.'

Thordric grinned, about to say that perhaps Vey should consider putting it on the council's production line, but then his face fell as he caught sight of the tree. Beside it, where the black orb had been, was a ball of tangled twigs and leaves.

Vey followed his gaze. 'That was what was under the orb's surface. It's the original spell,' he explained.

'It hasn't been broken yet?' Thordric said.

'No, it's the magic of the ancient Watchem Watchems. We can't touch it,' he replied.

Thordric let out a disgusted grunt. So, all they'd done was simply lift the magic that Kal had put on it?

'The Watchem Watchems here tried to break it while you were unconscious,' Hamlet said. 'But it looks as though they're not as powerful.'

A small whining came from the Watchem Watchems as he spoke and Thordric saw that they were all crying small tears of sap. He smiled at them. 'It's not your fault,' he said. 'We had no idea what we would find here. It's my fault for expecting so much of you all.'

They gurgled at him, looking slightly happier and started climbing onto his shoulders. Then he felt something hard hit his head and bounce across the floor. It was one of the crystals.

Glancing around to see who'd thrown it, he saw the elderly one staring. It pointed at him, then to itself and finally at the floating mass of twigs.

'I don't understand,' Hamlet said beside him. 'What is it trying to say?'

Thordric looked at it blankly. 'I'm not sure,' he said. Another crystal flew at his head. The Watchem Watchems sitting on him hissed angrily and knocked it away, hitting Hamlet instead. He yelled out in pain and the Watchem Watchems gurgled.

Thordric told them off and they went quiet.

The elderly one pointed again, in the same order, but still, he didn't understand.

'I think I do,' Vey said, nodding to the Watchem Watchem. 'It's trying to tell us to work together.'

'Can we do that?' Thordric asked.

'I can't see why not. If we form a chain with them like we do in normal group magic, then perhaps it will work.'

He stood up and, with Hamlet's help, lifted Thordric onto his feet. The Watchem Watchems stayed clinging to Thordric's tattered robes as he made his way slowly over to the floating ball of twigs and leaves.

There, they climbed down to his hands and hung there from one another, forming two small chains from his fingertips. The ones dangling from his right side pointed at Vey. Taking the hint, Vey took the hand of the one nearest the ground, lifting it up so that so that they all dangled between him and Thordric.

Seeing what they were trying to do, Hamlet took the hand of the lowest one on the other side. He felt the spiky fingers of the elderly one in his shin and, looking down, realised it wanted to be lifted too. Picking it up with his free hand, Vey then took hold of the elderly one's other hand, making the circle complete.

The other Watchem Watchems kicked their feet excitedly for a moment, dangling in the air, making Thordric, Hamlet and Vey's outstretched arms shake uncomfortably. Then the elderly one hissed loudly and they stopped.

'Will this work even though I'm part of it?' Hamlet asked nervously, looking at the two wizards.

Vey smiled. 'The magic will simply pass through you. What matters is that the chain remains strong. As long as you concentrate on that, it will be fine.'

Focusing on the floating ball of twigs, Thordric and Vey felt their magic merge with that of the Watchem Watchems. It was a curious sensation, and he suddenly felt as though he was connected to every bush, tree, and plant in the world. He could feel it all, living and growing around him. Risking a glance, he saw that Vey was pulling the same expression he was. So, he felt it as well.

The sensation grew, but then it narrowed down to just the forest growing above them. He could almost see the new saplings shooting up into adult trees. It felt as though they were being forced to grow and were crying out for help.

He wanted to return them back to the tiny seeds they had grown from and, hearing the Watchem Watchems gurgle encouragingly beside him, he concentrated his magic on trying to make it happen.

A few of the twigs in the floating ball snapped. He focused his magic more intensely, beads of sweat forming at his brow.

Swiftly, all the remaining twigs broke apart at once and the ball disintegrated onto the floor.

Breathing heavily, he, Vey and Hamlet set the Watchem Watchems back onto the ground and then sat down themselves, their energy spent.

A groaning sound made them jump. The tree was slowly changing colour and becoming smoother; its branches shaping into arms and hands while the middle one changed into a head and neck. The shards of the black orb that had been embedded in it dropped to the floor with a soft tinkling. Then the split trunk formed a pair of legs and, after a moment, a boy of around thirteen stood there, staring around the room, quite bewildered.

'Who are you people?' he asked, his voice croaking so much that they couldn't understand him. He coughed and asked again, though it was only slightly better.

For some reason, Hamlet and Vey both looked at Thordric to explain. He sighed and started at the beginning.

After making their way back up the tunnel, much easier now that Vey and Thordric could use their magic again, they came out at the main excavation site to find the archaeologists all sitting around, shaking their heads, and rubbing their eyes as though trying to shake off a good night's sleep. One of them had even found Hamlet's camping stove and kettle in the tent and was using it to make tea.

Thordric blinked as he looked around.

The trees had all vanished, though the Valley Flats were far from barren again. Small, delicate flowers covered the site like a carpet, spreading out as far as he could see. He looked at Vey suspiciously, but Vey shook his head and pointed to the elderly Watchem Watchem.

Thordric laughed and the others all gurgled happily, making the archaeologists stare.

Once they had explained everything again, everyone; Thordric, Vey, Hamlet, the boy Kal, the Watchem Watchems and the archaeologists; all boarded *Dinia's Jewel*.

It was a tight fit, with Hamlet and the Watchem Watchems once again piled in the single cabin together while everyone else tried to stay standing on deck, but soon they had sailed in sight of *The Jardine*.

Vey and Thordric opened the panel in *The Jardine's* hull and steered the ship inside, closing it again behind them. They summoned more fires lighting the cargo hold and, once the boat's levitation system had been deactivated, everyone disembarked.

'What about the Watchem Watchems?' Thordric asked Vey, as he watched them come out of the cabin with Hamlet, who was trying his best to ignore their sharp fingers as they poked at his feet.

'We'll return them to Watchem Woods on our way to Jard Town,' he replied. 'But first we need to help the people of Valley Edge fix their homes.'

. . .

'Goodness,' Morweena cried when she saw the state the three of them were in. 'What happened to you all?'

Thordric and Hamlet looked away awkwardly, but Vey smiled at her. 'We were simply making it safe for everyone to return to Valley Edge,' he said. 'I didn't wish to worry you with the details before we left, dear Auntie.'

'You stopped the forest?' Roomer asked, standing next to her.

'Yes...the trees are all gone, but the damage is still there,' Vey said.

'What about Tome and Yim?' he said anxiously.

Vey frowned. 'They must still be somewhere by the dig site. We didn't see them though, so perhaps they made their way back to your hideout. Either way, I'm sure they'll turn up sometime.' He turned to Thordric and Hamlet. 'Shall we get some breakfast? I'm terribly hungry after all of that.'

Thordric felt his stomach grumble as Vey spoke. Breakfast sounded like a wonderful idea to him.

They made their way down the corridor to the dining room, where several people were hurrying out looking decidedly startled.

As they got closer, they understood why.

A loud gurgling was coming from inside the room and, as Thordric opened the door, he saw the Watchem Watchems sitting around a large table, eating vegetables off a large platter in the centre.

Vey turned to him guiltily. 'I couldn't let them go hungry,' he said. 'Though I was surprised they like the same vegetables as we do.'

After filling their own plates, the three of them sat at the table too and ate their meal without anyone else coming in. The Watchem Watchems hissed slightly at the meat on their plates, but as soon as it was clear that they didn't have to eat it themselves, they went back to stabbing the vegetables with their spiny fingers and gobbling them into their mouths.

'What are you going to do with Kal?' Thordric asked after a while.

'He'll be coming back with us to be trained. His mother might be indifferent, but the captain was more than happy to hear that he was still alive. I believe that Kal and Lily are in the cabin with him now,' Vey replied.

'Are you going to get the inspector to charge him with anything though?' Thordric said.

Vey shook his head. 'He might have caused one of the biggest disasters that I've ever seen, but that still doesn't mean he needs to be punished. After all, if I'd had any sense and decided to come out here and let everyone know about the council's reform earlier, then this probably wouldn't have happened.'

He took a drink of blueberry and chocolate tea. 'I think you should be the one to teach him,' he said.

Thordric gaped. 'But I don't know enough yet.'

'I hardly know anything either, when you think about all the magic that's possible, and look at the position they gave me,' Vey said seriously, causing Thordric to snort.

Even Hamlet raised his eyebrows, for it was common knowledge that Vey knew more magic than the whole Council put together, despite only being in his late thirties and thus one of the youngest wizards there.

Vey ignored them both and continued. 'It's not about how much magic you don't know, but your experience with using the magic that you do know. In the few years that I've known you, you've built up great control, and *that* is precisely what Kal needs to learn.'

Thordric looked down at his plate. He supposed his control

was good, considering that he only really began to master his magic just over three years ago.

'Alright, I'll teach him everything I know,' he said at last. 'But I'll still get to train with you, won't I?'

'Of course,' Vey replied. 'I wouldn't want to waste your potential. Besides, mother would never speak to me again if I did.'

Thordric suddenly remembered something. 'Would it be alright if I taught Hamlet a few things too?' he said. 'I know he won't be able to use all the magic that we do, but I can teach him to make potions.'

Vey looked at him and then at Hamlet, stroking his beard thoughtfully. 'What an interesting idea,' he said at last. 'Assuming that you would like to?' he asked Hamlet.

Hamlet swallowed. 'Well, I...I've always wanted to be able to use magic,' he said, accidentally biting his tongue. 'I know I wasn't born a wizard, but Thordric said potions work from the magic of the ingredients, not the wizard making them.'

'They do; or at least a vast majority do,' Vey said. He paused. 'Yes, I think this is a very good idea. Perhaps we should ask others if they wish to learn potion making, too.'

26

A SURPRISE FOR HAMLET

The next morning, all the wizards onboard the fleet of the Ships of Kal helped to return the people of Neathin Valley back down to the ground.

It was much quicker than it had been getting them aboard, for, after their last group magic attempt, Vey decided it was stable enough to use on a regular basis. Despite her hints of wanting to go back to Jard Town with them to visit Lizzie, Morweena was one of the first to be lowered down.

High up as they were, everyone aboard still heard her shriek when she discovered the state of her house, despite the fact that Vey had explained to everyone that he personally would help out in the repair of the whole of Valley Edge.

The Watchem Watchems had come out on deck to watch all the goings on, having been given free run of the ship by Vey. As they were nervous around that many people, most of them had returned to being bushes. None of the people waiting to be lowered down could quite work out why there were so many plants onboard and so edged around them nervously. However, some of the Watchem Watchems were overcome with curiosity and couldn't help but shuffle along behind the people that were most wary, so Thordric had to deal with a few cases of people trying to climb the main mast in an attempt to get away from them.

After all that'd happened, he found he was enjoying doing such trivial things and, once or twice, he forgot to tell the Watchem Watchems that chasing people around was not good for the safety of everyone else.

As soon as all the people were back on the ground, Vey, Thordric and the other wizards lowered all the horses and other animals down as well, aside from Koleson who would remain on *The Jardine* until Thordric was back in Jard Town.

Finally, with Hamlet and Kal staying behind to rest some more, all of the wizards spread across the fleet descended down to Valley Edge themselves to assess the damage and see what they could do to help.

Naturally, Thordric and Vey were caught by Morweena the moment they stepped on the ground and were dragged into what remained of her house.

The hallway had been completely demolished, as had most of the lounge, so the only way to enter was through the kitchen, which had survived with the exception of missing one wall. Upstairs had fared no better, having collapsed completely, with all the books that Thordric had shrunk having returned to normal size, due to the power of the forest's magic, and were spilling down what remained of the staircase.

'Well, we've certainly got a lot of work to do,' Vey said, standing outside and assessing all of the damage at once. 'We need to raise the foundations first; the walls and ceilings of all the rooms downstairs. After that we should have a firm base to fix the second floor and the roof.'

Thordric nodded and went around to the side, directly outside the lounge.

'On my mark,' Vey said as Thordric stood ready. 'Now!'

Using magic on both sides, they heaved the bricks of the lounge back up into position to form the walls. Wetting the mortar that was already on them so the bricks stuck together once more, they then heated it so that it would dry out. They stood back a moment, seeing whether it would hold. It did.

Feeling encouraged, they did the same throughout the house. Within thirty minutes, the outside had been fully rebuilt. Now all they had to do was fix the inside and decorate, though, as Morweena kindly pointed out, the decorating should be Thordric's task as per the arrangement she had made in letting him stay there.

Vey, wanting to help the other wizards fix the rest of Valley Edge, clapped Thordric on the back rather cheerfully and left him to it.

'Don't forget about the mural you promised me,' Morweena said sweetly. Thordric remembered promising no such thing, but he did it anyway.

After decorating the bedrooms and the lounge in the most outrageous of colours as per her instruction, he found a blank space in the kitchen. It wasn't very big, but she seemed happy with the location and so he started to paint.

Focusing on a single spot on the wall, he thought of painting the outline of one of the houses. Colour spread out in lines as he pictured it and, now that he was warmed up enough, the whole of Valley Edge began to take shape. However, instead of how it had been before the forest had overtaken it, Thordric decided that he would paint the trees in too, rising high into the sky.

Finally, he painted in the Ships of Kal, floating in to rescue the people. When he was done, he stepped back to admire his handiwork. It looked how it did in his memory.

Just then Morweena came in and, with her, was Tome,

though to Thordric's surprise he wasn't using any disguise at all.

'Thordric, would you believe that this gentleman is called Tome as well?' she said, but then stopped, her eyes locked on the mural. Her necklaces all jangled about her neck as she bounced up to it for a closer inspection. 'I see what dear Lizzie was talking about; this is marvellous!'

Thordric wasn't listening. Instead, he was looking at Tome, who was staring back at him looking slightly confused.

'I was told that you might be able to help me,' Tome said, shifting uncomfortably. 'You see, I seem to have suffered a memory lapse and have no idea who I am other than my name.'

'Wait here for a moment,' Thordric said, unsure of whether he was lying. He decided Vey would be able to tell.

Dashing out of the house, he found Vey helping to rebuild Mr Henders' house around the corner. He saw that Mr Henders himself and his brother Grale were helping too, being slowly instructed by Vey on where to focus their magic.

Vey saw him and turned, apologising to the others, and telling them to keep at it.

'What is it, Thordric?' he asked as Thordric led him back to Morweena's.

'Tome has just turned up. He said he's lost his memory and has no idea who he is,' Thordric explained.

'Interesting,' Vey noted.

They went inside to where Morweena and Tome were still standing, looking at the mural. Vey saw it too and gave Thordric a nod of approval.

'Very nice, you've captured it perfectly,' he said, before turning to Tome. 'I understand that you've lost your memory, sir.'

'Indeed, Mr...?' Tome said, eyeing Vey up.

'Vey,' Vey replied. 'High Wizard of the Wizard Council.'

He studied Tome closely, inspecting his eyes in particular. 'Well, I don't think he's lying,' he said to Thordric.

Thordric blinked. 'Really? How can you tell?'

'Aside from his lack of reason to, his eyes seem rather glazed and unfocused,' Vey replied.

'And you can tell from that?' Thordric asked.

'No; we've just had a wizard named Yim arrive saying the exact same thing, though he wasn't even sure which part of the country he was in.'

'Yim turned into a tree too,' Thordric told him.

'I thought so. I suspect this memory loss is a temporary after effect. Both of them are much older than the other victims, so I suppose it stands to reason that they wouldn't come out of it quite so easily.'

Tome stared at them both, though Morweena seemed to have forgotten they were there. 'Are you both telling me that I was a tree?' he asked, his already white beard seeming to go even whiter.

'Indeed, sir,' Vey replied. 'But I'm afraid explanations will have to wait until Valley Edge has been fully repaired. 'For now, you can go with Thordric here back to our ship. Thordric, if you would?'

Thordric obliged and took Tome to *The Jardine,* where he found an empty cabin and locked him in it. Memory loss or not, Tome would still be questioned by Vey and the inspector once they got back to Jard Town.

Seeing as Vey had sent him back too, Thordric made his way to 'The Rookery' to check up on Hamlet. However, once he opened the door, he found that Lily, her brother Kal and all the Watchem Watchems were piled into the room with Hamlet squashed in the corner.

'What's going on here?' he asked, edging his way in. The Watchem Watchems gurgled and tried to climb up his robes.

'Kal was explaining how he managed to get to the magic underground,' Hamlet said, his voice somewhat strained from being squashed in place by everyone else.

Kal, who was perched on Thordric's bed next to Lily, blushed. 'I watched the archaeologists uncover those pyramid things and saw that they were the same shape as those two slots in the ground. I guessed they were some kind of keys and when I put them in after everyone else had gone, the slab opened up,' he said, rather pompously. 'So, I went down there and found that ball of floating twigs. I could feel a strange magic coming from it and I spent all night trying to harness it. Then the next morning, after I realised that those idiots must have taken the pyramids out again and trapped me inside, I gave up and threw every bit of magic at it that I could. After that I don't remember anything until I saw you down there.'

Thordric sighed, hoping that Kal wouldn't try anything so idiotic while he was teaching him.

The Jardine sailed into Jard Town a few days later, after Valley Edge had been completely rebuilt and the Watchem Watchems returned to the Watchem Woods.

As the mooring lines were tied to the docks and the boarding platform set into place, Thordric saw his mother and the inspector waiting for him, holding his two sisters. Lizzie was there also, watching the ship with a soft smile on her lips.

Vey had told her they'd be arriving, using his long-distance communicator, and she had obviously let the others know. As Thordric waved to them, Hamlet came up beside him, completely downcast. 'My mother's down there too,' he said, pointing to a woman dressed from neck to toe in stiff, formal clothing. Next to her was a tall, wide man with short grey hair and a goatee beard. He had a look of distaste on his face as he glanced up and saw Hamlet.

'Who is that next to her?' Thordric asked, taking an instant dislike to the man.

'That's my professor. I doubt he expected me back so soon,' Hamlet replied.

Thordric looked at him, remembering that he'd said he thought his professor had designs on his mother. 'What are you going to do now?' he asked.

Hamlet shrugged. 'Now that I'm back, I'll be graduating in a few weeks. After that, I'm not sure.'

They got ready to disembark. Lily, who had decided to stay on the ship with her father to see her brother safely to Jard town, ran to Thordric and pulled on his sleeve. Before he could say anything however, she simply thrust an apple in his hand and ran off again.

He stared after her, seeing Kal, Tome and Vey come out of the captain's cabin and make their way down the platform to the docks below. Mr Henders; now with his hand and back normal again thanks to Vey's magic; and his brother, Grale, also came out from the cabin and followed them down.

Shrugging, Thordric and Hamlet disembarked as well, parting once they reached the docks to meet up with their families.

As he picked up his sisters and let them tug at his hair and beard, Thordric saw Hamlet's mother scolding him on his appearance, which admittedly was much less well kempt than it had been when Thordric had first met him. He saw Hamlet look at the ground, slowly reddening as his professor decided to berate him too.

Thordric scowled at them, but caught Lizzie watching him curiously.

'There seems to be something troubling you, boy,' she said

softly. 'Why don't you give the twins to me and see if you can sort it out.'

He blinked, but then caught her meaning.

Handing her the twins, he went over to Vey, who was discussing Tome with the inspector. He interrupted, apologising, and asked Vey for a word.

Vey stepped aside, a questioning look on his face. Thordric quickly explained his idea and the look changed to one of approval, and the High Wizard sent him off with an encouraging wave.

Hamlet was making to leave with his mother and the professor when Thordric caught up with them.

'Who in Spell's name are you?' the professor asked, obviously missing the council's symbol on Thordric's robes.

'I am Wizard Thordric of the council, sir,' he replied formally. 'I have come to speak with your student here.'

'You want something of Hamlet?' Hamlet's mother said, her voice as stiff as her clothing.

'Yes, ma'am. It seems that the Wizard Council is in need of assistance in a certain matter,' Thordric said.

'What matter?' the professor said, while Hamlet looked at him speechlessly.

'There are specific documents in our library that contain details of ancient magical objects. Unfortunately, none of our wizards have the time nor the expertise to uncover such things, so High Wizard Vey has requested Hamlet's help in the matter,' Thordric said. 'He was invaluable to us in helping clear up the disaster in Neathin Valley. I'm afraid everything has already been decided. Hamlet will come with us. We have already allocated a room for him and shall be collecting the rest of his belongings in the morning.'

Everyone stared at him.

'Hamlet, if you would kindly come with High Wizard Vey

and me back to the council, we shall brief you on everything,' he continued, rather enjoying himself.

'I...certainly, Wizard Thordric,' Hamlet replied, before saying goodbye to his mother and the professor, who, Thordric noticed, were gaping slightly.

They walked away, back to where Vey and Thordric's family still stood.

'What you said just now,' Hamlet began. 'Was it true?'

Thordric grinned. 'Mostly,' he said. 'Besides, it got you away from them, didn't it?'

Hamlet smiled. Perhaps his future wouldn't be so bad after all.

Dear reader,

We hope you enjoyed reading *Accidental Archaeologist*. Please take a moment to leave a review, even if it's a short one. Your opinion is important to us.

Discover more books by Kathryn Wells at https://www.nextchapter.pub/authors/kathryn-wells-fantasy-author

Want to know when one of our books is free or discounted? Join the newsletter at http://eepurl.com/bqqB3H

Best regards,
Kathryn Wells and the Next Chapter Team

The story continues in:
Unseasoned Adventurer

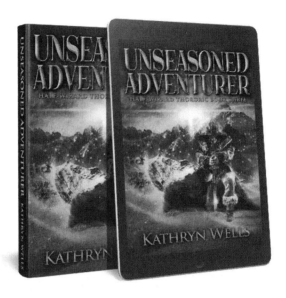

To read the first chapter for free, please head to:
https://www.nextchapter.pub/books/unseasoned-adventurer-
middle-grade-fantasy-adventure-kathryn-wells

ABOUT THE AUTHOR

Kathryn Wells is the pen name of author Kathryn Rossati, a writer of fantasy, children's fiction, short stories, and poetry.

As a child, she found her passion for the written word, and even though she had many other interests growing up, writing was always the one she would return to.

Her favourite authors are Diana Wynne Jones, Geanna Culbertson, Suzanne Collins, Jonathan Stroud, Neil Gaiman, Garth Nix, and David Eddings, to name but a few.

You can find more information about Kathryn on her website:

http://www.kathrynrossati.co.uk

BOOKS BY THE AUTHOR

Unofficial Detective (Half-Wizard Thordric Book 1)
Accidental Archaeologist (Half-Wizard Thordric Book 2)
Unseasoned Adventurer (Half-Wizard Thordric Book 3)
The Door Between Worlds

Printed in Great Britain
by Amazon

69170281R00130